Pay Back

A Charlie Ford Adventure

Book Two

By Mike Evans

To all my fans and supporters, thank you for still loving to read this near and dear to my heart.
****

This Book is licensed for your personal enjoyment upon purchase. Thanks for respecting this author's work.

Thank you for reading! I do hope that you enjoy it!

© 2022 Mike Evans, All Rights Reserved

Edited by Elizabeth Robbins Editing Services

I would like to thank my special team of beta readers, these folks are amazing, Leslie and Karen.

You can find all things Mike Evans related at

MIKE EVANS AUTHOR WEBSITE
https://www.mikeevansauthor.com/

Mike's newsletter don't miss out on any news! I will NOT SPAM YOU.
http://www.tinyurl.com/evansnews

Mike Evans Facebook Author Page
https://www.facebook.com/MikeEvansAuthor

Contact Email
m.evansauthor@gmail.com

Mike Evans on Amazon
https://www.amazon.com/Mike-Evans/e/B00IQ9Z75A

Stand-alone and Series by Mike Evans

Charlie Ford Adventure Series
The Orphans Series
Gabriel Series
The Uninvited Series
Demons Beware Series
Zombies and Chainsaws
Zombies on The Block Series
Deal with The Devil
Buried: Broken oaths
Voices in My Head
The Operator

Chapter 1

Charlie was pretty damn sure that it was going to either be now or never if he wanted to try and do something to free himself. He knew that the cement did not have much longer and was pretty happy about the fact that the two dumb shits had not used quick-drying cement. He was not in the business of being a thug, so he thought that it was going to have to be something that they learned on their own. It wasn't the kind of job advice he felt like offering people at all.

Bruno didn't have much of an issue lifting up Charlie. In hindsight, had Bruno known everything that was going to happen after this, he would have happily just bear-hugged Charlie and dead-lifted him or at least dragged him over to the edge of the boat. Charlie kept his head down and knew that the man on the left was unquestionably Lou. His small arms and hands made that quite easy to differentiate him from the gorillas that he ran with in his crew. Charlie's head was swinging left and right, but he could see the pistol tucked inside Lou's waistband holster.

It didn't take long, once they got moving, to get to the edge of the boat's deck. He knew that this would be his end once they made it to the edge of the ship. That now or never thing quite frankly was screaming at the absolute top of its lungs at him to move and to do so now! As they inched forward, getting closer by the second, Charlie waited until he could see the water. Lou said, "I'll hold his top and you lift the cement bucket."

Bruno was looking at the cement noticing one thing, and that was that it had not completely set. Bruno said, "When I told you to run in and grab a couple of bags of this, did you get the quick dry? Because this cement here does not look hardened, even in the moonlight. It looks like it's loose. What do you think was gonna happen when we go and toss this wet cement bucket into the very wet water, Lou?"

Charlie whispered, "I'm pretty sure that he got the cement which takes a long time to dry."

Bruno wasn't looking up but began answering before realizing unless it was Lou that he shouldn't be hearing any voices. Bruno replied, "Yeah, god damn it."

Bruno had to think about it before he could react to it because, quite frankly, he was an idiot. The moment he realized that Charlie was awake, he started rising to his feet as quickly as he could. Charlie, at this point, was not going to feel too damn guilty about anything that happened to these two buffoons. He was not really a huge fan of revenge, but as of right now, he had been kidnapped against his will. He was quite confident that these two had killed his only remaining living relative. Not that he really needed to add anything else, but they'd wasted his time, and really, quite frankly, fucking pissed him off. Charlie would not waste another moment as a captive if he did not need to.

Charlie leaned over before Lou had had a chance, much like Bruno, to put everything together. The moment Lou attempted to move away was exactly when Charlie leaned over, realizing all he had at the moment available to him was his mouth, his head, and unfortunately as little as he wanted to do it…his teeth. Charlie put everything that went along with it so he could do what he needed to. Charlie hoped he wouldn't catch anything and leaned over gripping tightly, clenching his teeth onto Lou's ear. Lou screamed as Charlie wasted zero time with his clenched mouth looking like a puppy with a rag toy shaking his head furiously left and right.

Lou cried for help, "Bruno, fucking shoot him! He's got my god damn ear!"

Bruno was already pulling his pistol when Charlie finished and was happy that there were no bones in an ear. Charlie had ripped off half of his ear from what remained. To make matters worse, Charlie spit the ear in front of him and into the ocean. His mouth was covered with blood, and he looked like he could be an extra in a zombie movie. Lou was going to say something else, but Charlie brought his head back, and then forward as hard as he could. Lou was still trying to figure out what to do about his ear, not seeing Charlie thrusting forward as hard as he absolutely could directly into Lou's face.

Lou might have been the only one on the day they had broken into his boat before reinforcements had come to be able to not leave with a broken nose. This anomaly out of him and his fellow mob-like individuals was now over. Charlie had held nothing back and if he had not had his hands tied behind his back, he would have done a hell of a lot fucking more if he could have. But that wasn't the case; at least not yet anyways.

Lou went to grip onto his nose when Charlie, who still was not
done, brought his head up hitting him directly under his chin, and
clipped it just enough so that when Lou went to say something,
the tip of his tongue fell out, landing on the boat deck. He
immediately realized that he had a lisp. Bruno was still getting up
to his feet. His generous size was handy, but at the same time, it
could lead to situations where agility, or the lack thereof, would
be a downfall. Just as he was trying to get up, the ocean lent a
hand to Charlie. It was a gift horse that he would not look in the
mouth.

A wave seemed to come from nowhere out of the darkness of
night. It hit the boat's front, sending it up four feet. Bruno fell
backward, losing his grip on Charlie, and hit his head quite hard
on the boat's deck. Charlie knew that right now was probably as
good a time as any to try and get his feet free. Charlie lost his
balance for a minute seeing a light blue light thinking there was
no fucking way at all this could be true. He lifted the cushion with
his head, seeing the light was a phone. Charlie backed up to it
awkwardly until he could grab it, and slid it into his front pocket,
and then went for his original item. However, the thing that he
really wanted was to get something a little bit more useful to fight
back with than his mouth and forehead. Charlie pushed back into
Lou, his hands moving around his waist like a virgin on prom night
before finally finding exactly what it was that he had been looking
for.

Charlie didn't know if he'd ever been so happy as when he had found Lou's pistol and quickly gripped onto it, pulling it back until he freed it out of its holster. Charlie did not need to look; he immediately found the safety on the gun and from there still wasn't feeling amazing about being out in the middle of the fucking ocean with two goons. But regardless, it was still better than the circumstances were previously. One thing Charlie realized was aiming was not really an option when the gun was behind you, but he sure as shit would be more than able to fire off a few shots.

Charlie took those few rounds, not hitting anything, or if he had struck something it apparently didn't hit anything that hurt enough for either man to scream in agony. Right now, that would have very much been something he'd be happy to hear. However, it did make Lou jump back a few feet and Bruno rolled over, for some reason thinking Charlie would have an issue shooting a guy that kidnapped him in the back but that was not the case.

Charlie fell backward, lifting (or more so fighting) to get his feet out of the mixture. It had somewhat set, but not enough to fully trap him in a full bucket. Charlie tried to kick the rest of the cement off, but some of it was not going anywhere without help. Charlie was a strong swimmer, but he also was not an idiot; treading water was largely successful because of kicking your feet, and that was going to be an exercise that he could only do for so long. If he survived this crazy-ass night, getting the cement off would be his next most important task. Charlie really hoped that it ended in his favor versus the alternative. That he knew what could happen.

 When Charlie was on the deck, he went to bring his feet up and try to get his hands out from behind his back. Both men seemed quite aware of what would happen if a very pissed-off and armed guy was able to free himself. Bruno yelled the obvious, "He needs to be off of this goddamn boat!"

Lou lisped, "No swit supid."

Charlie never worried about putting salt on an open wound, laughing, "Uh, you're sounding a little bit like Mike Tyson there. Why is that; do you think?"

Bruno yelled, "Keep laughing it up, motherfucker. Once this ends, you'll see exactly what is coming your way."

Charlie had almost gotten his legs free when Bruno took hold of him by the crotch and shirt, lifting him up and over his head before launching him five feet off the boat's side. Charlie took a deep breath as he hit the water, and as he was trying to think of a plan, still thought getting his feet under him would be great because then he could get his hands in front of him as well which felt like an excellent idea for swimming and or floating.

Charlie hit the water sucking in a deep breath. He knew this shit wasn't completely hardened and that it might take a second or two to free his feet of more of it or at least enough to be able to use his feet for something more than an anchor. Charlie had done a deep dive quickly before, but this was something different; this was faster than he'd ever gone down before. Charlie pushed his first foot down while pulling the other up. In that time, he figured he was thirty feet deep, and with every second ticking by he was going to get even deeper. It wasn't going to get any better any time soon. By the time he got both of his legs back, he began kicking as much as he could. Charlie strained to even see the moonlight from that far down.

Each of his legs felt like whatever cement was left was adding an extra ten or twenty pounds, maybe more, he didn't know. Charlie kicked and looked like a mad man using his arms to pull himself up faster by the second. When he broke through from what felt like a mile below water, he sucked in a breath that felt like someone had placed a flamethrower in his mouth and pulled the trigger. Charlie again wasn't going to point out the obvious to these dipshits, but if they'd put a chain around his waist and then done his handcuffs through the chain, he would have never made it back up to the water's surface.

The boat hadn't moved more than a few feet. He couldn't really say for sure, mostly because he didn't know if he was going at an angle or not. The two of them looked surprised to see him. Secretly, both men had hoped the cement was done setting enough to never have to see Charlie Ford again. Charlie now had his hands where they could do something and fired off three more shots, not stopping until he, unfortunately, ran out of ammunition.

Charlie's shoulders slumped when he clicked on empty. They didn't know he was out and obviously when he'd been stealing the gun in the first place, he'd not thought about getting an extra magazine. It had been a huge but temporary victory just getting the gun in the first place and getting most of the cement block off his feet. Charlie was well aware that he had to try to figure out what the fuck he would do now.

Charlie figured pretty quickly that they didn't feel like exchanging gunfire. As well there wasn't anything that would lead them to believe he would survive this. Charlie felt confident that was their plan because he watched as they gunned the engines, racing off. Charlie watched, overjoyed that they were not staying around. A direction he hoped they would continue with and really didn't want them to turn around and come back his way.

Charlie tucked the empty pistol in his pocket and looked around, trying to find the North Star, not extremely happy about one simple fact which was it was not a completely cloud-free evening. He squinted, trying to make out the star that would be his compass and savior, leading him back to shore. When he did, he questioned how far he would have to go before he could make it back to shore. It wouldn't sadden him if at some point the concrete began coming off of his legs. Charlie was doing his best to float on his back but was too bottom-heavy at the moment to do a very good job of it. He saw lights coming in his direction and immediately assumed the absolute worst, which was the seeming safe bet for this shit show of a day. Charlie very much wondered if they were coming back, intent on mowing him down with the boat's engine. Charlie was confident they weren't sharp shooters with these at all.

The crew of four had pinpointed where Charlie was when they'd seen the boat. Unfortunately, they did not know where to go once the boat went in one direction and his signal stayed where the boat had been. Cliff, who had not in any way volunteered to go on this boat ride said, "I don't know which way we should go?"

Tim said, "I'm taking the water; you guys go after that boat. I've got my phone handy. Do me a favor: if I call you, come back and fucking get us. If he isn't on that boat, well, come back and fucking get me. That is not a question. It's a fact in a fucking statement."

Jim, always the smartass, said, "Oh, so you get the easy job of jumping in the water swimming over and finding out that he's not there, or maybe he is?"

Tim shrugged saying, "We really don't have time for this, Jim. Would you rather jump into the cool ass water and swim over to see if our buddy Charlie's alive and well, or stay on the boat?"

Jim was thinking of the alternative when Tim decided he did not have time to wait for Jim's smartass answer or decision. Tim turned around, grabbed an inflatable life vest from the side of the boat storage, and raced off, leaping headfirst into a perfect dive, and disappearing beneath the darkness of the night's waters. Jim tried to squint as if somehow that would actually help, but of course, it didn't, and his dark skin didn't help to define where he was beneath the water. He didn't waste any time though when he came up and looked like he might give an Olympic swimmer a run for their money.

Tim was moving as fast as he possibly could. He just hoped that Charlie was okay, it was extremely rare for him to ask anyone for help. He knew that hardheadedness was something that Charlie had zero lack of. Tim didn't let up for a second, going as fast as he could to where he hoped he would find his friend and not just more of the darkness of night.

Cliff was looking around the boat, debating if maybe he should just jump off with a life jacket of his own and pray that a shark didn't eat his ass while swimming home. He did not care for the prospect of being shot at, and he would not be amazed if Bruno and Lou thought that that was an intelligent idea.

Johnney could see the nervousness in Cliff's face as well as his movement and he said, "You can jump, kid. However, unless you'd like to swim 25 or 30 miles, you're nowhere near land. Nothing personal, but I really think that you might be smart to just stay here. Your choice, grab a life jacket if you think that is the intelligent way to go. Your chances of getting shot at will probably be a lot less.

Cliff took a hard good look at the deep, dark water, watching the waves and patting a stomach that wasn't fat but sure as hell didn't resemble the other two that he was close in age to, but not physique, and realized staying on the boat, at least until all shit hit the fan, was probably the safer idea. Cliff was still looking at the tracker system on the phone saying, "They either dumped him or the phone in the water. It's impossible to tell, but something had to have happened."

Johnney said to Jim, "You take the shotgun, and you can go sit on the front of the boat. I like to mix things up when I've got trouble. So, listen here; your first two are birdshot, and the last three are slugs. I don't care what kind of boat that is, outside of maybe being a Naval ship, there's not much that's gonna stop those slugs when they get moving. So, you just make sure you aim straight and true, and I'm going to get you up on their ass. If they start shooting, I'll hold her straight, but if you want me to turn off, just raise up your fist with your left hand and we can call that good for a signal."

Jim didn't know if good would be the right phrase to use for that, but by God, he was going to do his best to at least try and stick with this as long as he needed to. Just like Tim, Jim knew how little Charlie asked for help, he actually didn't even know that it was in his vocabulary to do so. He didn't know how many times he had helped out a friend, especially when Tim had missed the point spread on a bet by more than a few points and didn't have the money on hand to pay the ship's bookie that took action on the side. Charlie had made it crystal clear to the ship's personal bookie that after they'd had to help Tim out with a hefty bill that if he ever under any circumstances was ignorant enough to let him place another bet that Charlie would make it his absolute life fucking mission to make his life aboard that ship a complete and utter hell.

Jim stayed low, duck-walking up to the front of the boat's bow. He wasn't ignorant and knew they'd have to be pretty damn close, especially for the birdshot to hit anything. As they were inching closer by the second, the obvious power of Charlie's boat aka his home, made that job all that much easier. The only downside of this speed was it did nothing to take away from the bashing the boat was taking from cutting in, hitting waves hard. Jim had been on plenty of rough boats before. This wasn't an issue, although it was the first time he had been required to use a shotgun at the same time.

Jim saw the explosion from the muzzle before he heard it. The pistol looked like he was lighting off a warning flare with each squeeze of the gun's trigger. The shitty thing for Jim was that he had to worry about hitting Charlie...given he was on the boat in the first place. Lou and Bruno didn't seem to need to worry about this at all. They were happy as shit at getting to shoot and hitting Charlie's boat.

Jim waited until they hit a light patch of water and fired off the first two shells filled to the brim with birdshot. He aimed not so much at the boat but a few feet above where that muzzle flash was originating from. Jim was quite confident that he had hit something when the muzzle flash pointed straight up at the sky. Jim knew these little pellet shots weren't going to kill anything that wasn't a bird or critter, but by God, it was still going to sting like a son of a bitch if he did hit them. He smiled, feeling a little accomplishment from that. He knew whoever he'd hit with the pellets would be feeling and healing from that for a few days.

Jim looked back behind him, making sure and hoping that there'd been no direct hits with the pistol. He assumed they were shooting in his direction, but there weren't any holes to prove such a thing. Jim figured they were having as hard of a time shooting as he was. There was nothing you could do with those boats to keep it steady when they were going, especially at these speeds. A pissed-off Johnney was manning the boat still and he couldn't see Cliff, but he was pretty confident that he had probably dived for the floor when he had heard the first gunshots going off. Johnney knew, in his defense, the guy really didn't have a whole lot invested in Charlie or them, so the idea of risking his life for any of these people was probably a little bit more than what he felt was required of doing a good deed.

***

Lou had just been focused on what was in front of them. He also was trying to keep his head down, not wanting to catch a bullet in the rear of his head, or given his luck today, his ass. Lou yelled, "Bruno, fuckin keep shooting! They're catching up! What are you doing back there?"

Bruno turned around, his left cheek soaked in blood, tears coming out of his left eye, the light glistening from the blood. Lou could see where the skin had actually bubbled from the heat of the pellets as they burned their way into his cheek and bone. Lou was going to say something, but Bruno staggered forward, trying to keep his balance. Bruno handed him the gun, realizing he probably wasn't going to be much help for a couple of minutes.

Bruno pulled an extra magazine saying, "Shoot the motherfuckers! Then we go back and find that son of a bitch! I'm gonna run over his head with the propeller…repeatedly."

Lou didn't want to tell him how slim the chances would be of finding Charlie in the dark oceans. Especially given the fact they didn't have a clue where he had jumped from. It was not like they'd had coordinates where they'd gone to. It was just them going and stopping. Lou was trying to fire while driving. He knew giving Bruno a few minutes wouldn't hurt anything. Lou yelled, "Why don't you do something to help us besides getting shot and bleeding, dammit! This'll end badly for the two of us!"

Lou was going to say something else, but a very easy-to-read Bruno seemed to advise him that if he did say something then he'd probably have to worry about being killed by him. Bruno practically threw Lou to the side, taking the wheel of the boat and currently wishing that the two of them had had a machine gun. This whole thing was supposed to be pretty goddamn easy. Make the cement, let it set, dump asshole into the water, and then from there everything was gonna be gravy. Of course, this was not how anything had gone. This was really turning into a day from hell.

Lou was firing shots and doing his best not to fall over the side of the fucking boat. He yelled back to Bruno, who he knew wouldn't know the, but regardless felt justified in asking, "How in the fuck did they find us out in the middle of nowhere? I won't bring up the fact that if we had gone as far out as we were supposed to, we probably would have beaten them there, dumped him, and never had any issues."

Bruno screamed from the wheel yelling, "You do realize when you bit the end of your tongue off was the end of me being able to understand a goddamn thing that you said, right?"

Lou quickly and without hesitation gave him the middle finger, feeling the tip of his tongue which was only equal to pain from his broken nose and throbbing wound on his ear. He did not enjoy any of this shit. Bruno screamed, "Should we play chicken with them?"

Lou had to take a minute just to figure out if he was truly that stupid to ask such an idiotic question. He responded over the engine that was screaming going full bore not meant to be abused like this, "Are you fucking stupid? No, we should not play chicken! If that's Ford's boat, it's probably twice as long as ours and was actually meant to be out in the rough sea. It would probably go right through us and not even have to take a fucking breath."

"Are you sure?"

"No, that's why I say we probably shouldn't do that. The last thing I want to do is end up like that stupid fuck going overboard and be trapped out here in the middle of nowhere with absolutely no one coming in our direction to try and find us. I mean unless that's what floats your boat. Is that what you want to do?"

Bruno thought about the cold water, and how he wasn't much of a swimmer, and couldn't think of anyone in their life that liked them enough to come to search the open waters for them. Bruno shook his head no, yelling, "Just use those bullets!"

It only took a few more shots before Lou realized just how little of an impact he was having with this goddamn handgun. Lou just hoped that they could keep enough distance ahead of them that there would be a much lesser chance for fear of them catching up and killing them. He knew that that is exactly what they would do if they had more than just one handgun between the two of them. Also, the fact that both of them were very far from one hundred percent had not slipped his mind.

Lou knew that regardless of how this shit show of a day ended, it was not going to go well when they had to go back and tell Nydegger about the shitstorm that, not purposely, of course, had happened. They weren't scared so much of him but figured he had someone up above that would be much more upset and able to enforce it without any work. He kept doing his best to shoot toward Jim and the crew.

***

Jim knew that they were getting closer by the second, and he had used the two buckshot and was more than content to fire a slug off in their vicinity. Johnney screamed from the glass behind him. "Is there a reason that you aren't shooting those motherfuckers?" Jim turned around yelling, and pointing, "Go faster, get closer,"

He mouthed as well as he could knowing it was almost impossible to hear.

Johnney gave a thumbs up and almost rolled Jim backward a few feet when he gave it everything he could. Jim held steady to the metal chrome that surrounded the deck of the boat, doing his best to not literally take a dive. Jim knew that the fact that Charlie had already seemed to have issues with the police in town would not lend itself kindly to helping them beat a murder charge if they or in his case right now he shot and killed one of these two dumb asses on the boat. Truly little was ideal about anything that was going on. However, Jim was pretty sure he had an idea that would make the chase be done, as well as not having to worry about any murder charges coming his way.

Jim waited until they hit a smooth patch of water. He had the shotgun bead, which thankfully was pretty easy to see, given the fact that the boat he was aiming at was as white as fresh snow. When he felt they were close enough, and he was confident in his aim, Jim squeezed the trigger lovingly and gently.

The slug from the 12-gauge shotgun raced across the dark ocean waters. Jim watched, hoping, and praying that the shot would be true and would strike home where it needed to. The slug did exactly as expected and buried itself five inches deep in the engine. The boat they'd been chasing for a while would now finally come to a stop, he thought. It was not an easy thing to see, however, after a minute, the boat without question lost a serious amount of speed. These boats were not meant for coasting, as well the fact that there were waves which they were going into made that even less friendly for them to do any sort of long-distance coasting. His second clue was the rolling smoke that was coming from it.

Jim smiled as he watched the smoke rise from the engine and waited, knowing pretty confidently that their boat was not going to continue at this pace for very damn long. He couldn't have been more correct because Johnney, who had been paying attention but not quite as much as he probably should have, had to veer the boat when he realized that Jim had successfully taken out their engine. He missed it by inches, sending Lou and Bruno back and forth, fighting to keep their balance after the waves struck them.

Johnney yelled from behind the wheel, "You shot the fucking engine! I thought you were going to shoot the goddamn people on the boat!"

Jim screamed back, "One of those lands my ass in jail, the other one keeps me out of jail. I'm too goddamn pretty to go to jail!"

At the moment, Johnney was still pretty damn pissed-off about his boat dock having someone set off an explosion on it. So, unlike Jim, he was currently just seeing red at the moment and had nothing but intentions of death for anyone coming between him and his revenge. Jim could sense the anger and knew that it was probably a good thing he was the one shooting. When they made it up to the boat, the two men came out puffed up. Lou was aiming his pistol at Jim, who unfortunately for Lou was not an idiot. Jim smiled, actually laughing, yelling, "What in the hell do you plan on doing with that?"

"It's a gun, you stupid shit. What do you think that I'm gonna do?"

"Well unless you've got a reason that slide is back, I don't think you're gonna do a goddamn thing with it. I mean, outside of maybe throwing it at me."

Bruno who was always the tough guy but not necessarily so much the scholar snapped back, "You better watch how you talk to me!"

Jim just kind of sat there for a moment, waiting for the next sentence to come. But of course, there was no next sentence because he did not actually have something to add to that threat. Jim, who would have loved to have screwed with this guy, especially knowing he could basically say any damn thing he wanted to at this moment but knew getting back to the point of things was going to be more important than anything, and it pained him. Jim replied, "That's a mighty big threat you've got there, Bruno. Tell you what; we can stop talking, and you can give Charlie back to us."

"We're not giving anyone back to you!" Lou yelled or tried to yell but came back with more of a lisp than he would have liked to have.

Jim was noticing that since they'd last met, Lou had definitely taken the brunt of the damage and he could only assume Charlie had been the one who was lucky enough to inflict it on him. Jim asked, "You're not gonna give him back because you don't have him? ' Or you're not going to give him back because you guys think that you are tough assholes, who still have a bargaining chip?"

Bruno, never the thinker, said, "We are tough assholes!"

Jim smiled nodding, saying, "Yes, if a few war wounds make you tough assholes, then you guys are probably the biggest assholes I can think of in my book. What with your matching broken noses, gangster suits, with a side of someone never being able to say spaghetti without sounding like a little kid again. Oh, and with a chunk of ear missing wondering if Tyson was around and hungry?"

The two of them were fuming, but neither could do a goddamn thing about it. Quite frankly, it really, really pissed them off to no end. Johnney slid the window open yelling, "Do they have Charlie or not?"

Jim said, "I don't know. They're being assholes about it."

Johnney grabbed one of the pistols from inside the cabin and walked up, definitely looking like he was ready to kill and was not in any way or form in a fucking around mood about it. Johnney yelled, "You got five seconds to give us the kid, or I'm going to put half of this magazine in your face and the other half in yours. Luckily, only these two and God are going to be witnesses, so it'll be just about like you guys disappeared off the face of the earth. If there was an issue with police, well I feel like a few of these bullet holes would suffice us shooting."

Johnney started counting down, "five, four, three no one is going to miss either of you, one…"

Bruno surprisingly was the one that broke. Apparently, he thought he had something to live for. He yelled, "Stop. Don't. Just wait. Relax, that psycho jumped off the fucking boat."

Cliff said from the safety of the cockpit, "See, that's why the signal went the other way."

Both men realized these guys were just a little bit higher tech than they were and had led them to being found. Lou bent down slowly, picking up a rope saying, "Give us a tow in."

Johnney snorted and started laughing hard, "You guys want us to help you?"

Lou, not really considering the severity of the situation with having guns pointed at them out in the middle of the ocean, said, "Well that sure as fuck seems like about the only option we have, isn't it?"

Johnney asked, "So, you're saying you guys don't have a phone between the two of you?"

They shrugged, nodding, and Johnney fired off all ten rounds, being happy to share where he put those rounds across the entire side of the boat facing them. Lou and Bruno stepped forward seeing little air bubbles coming up quite quickly and letting the two men know that their time above water was probably going to be limited.

 Johnney looked at Cliff saying, "Put it in reverse. Get away from these guys."

Lou said, "You sure this is how you want to end things?"

Johnney said, "The only reason we're not killing you is because this redheaded feller thinks that he would have something to worry about if we did."

Jim, not a big fan of repeating himself said sarcastically, "Well I'm very sorry, Johnney, that I don't want to spend my last years of living in a jail considering I'm not ninety years old."

"Who the hell said I was 90 fucking years old? Jesus, how old do you think I am, you little ginger-headed shitball prick?"

Jim knew they kind of needed to get moving and said, "Well ninety is kind of what I thought."

Cliff said, "Don't you guys think maybe we should try to get back to the other guy and Charlie?"

Johnney smiled, walking back to the boat wheel, saying over his shoulder, "Well I sure hope you guys have good reception out here. Because I bet you got less than a half-hour before that fucker sinks."

Bruno, who probably should have shut up, tried to yell, sounding furious, but his cheek had puffed up looking like someone had cut it open, sewn a baseball in it, and then attacked the shit out of his cheek with a fork. Bruno said, "You just wait until we get back to land."

Johnney stopped dead in his tracks, turning around and taking the shotgun from Jim, holding it up and saying, "Because why? You two stupid fucks can't seem to do anything. So, what exactly is it that I am supposed to be scared of? The chances are, all that blood's gonna draw in sharks, and your stupid asses are going to get eaten. I can only hope by the pecker first. It's always good to have a small appetizer before a meal."

Jim realized if this guy was like sixty years younger it very well could be a younger or same version of himself. Bruno wanted to say something, but Lou hit him in the gut whispering, "Just shut the fuck up so they leave. We need to call for help."

Bruno said, "Fuck it."

The two turned around walking away, turning their backs on the shotgun and Johnney. For good measure Johnney fired off two more shots in less than a second, doing quite a bit more damage as the slug from the shotgun had struck the boat, and the slugs had opened on impact, taking more wood and fiberglass with it than the two men would have liked.

Cliff started backing up the boat, turning it around and headed straight in the direction of the signal. He hoped that they would find someone, or even better, find someone alive to make some of this somewhat worth it. Cliff did not love the idea that payback and retribution could be coming his way, and that he would be one of the ones held responsible for this shit show.

Chapter 2

Tim was swimming furiously as if his life or Charlie's life was dependent on it. He was not a die-hard workout guru, fitness-conscious, tofu-eating kind of guy. However, he did like it when his body could do the things that he was requesting from it. Tim, for the life of him, knew until he found Charlie that he did not need to quit swimming. He was straining to listen as he was going arm over arm, rotating his head so that he could breathe and hear, but that was growing difficult, given the fact that he had to bring up that ear that had just been in the water. Tim hoped that all this effort to help find his friend would be rewarded with finding him alive.

Tim was trying to make himself stop thinking negatively about the worst-case scenario. He was not a pessimist, but typically the only time he thought more about the fact that he couldn't fail was when he was playing with lady luck and hoping his team would cover the over-under which was always his favorite go-to.

Tim quit and just coasted for a moment, trying to listen, not quite sure what he would hear. He sure as shit didn't hear any engines, which meant at the moment he was going to be all on his lonesome for a few. Tim treaded water, trying to listen before finally hearing no shortage of cursing coming just a little bit off in the distance. He couldn't pinpoint exactly where it was, but he did know more than likely it was not far.

He heard that cursing again, followed by what sounded like the slapping of water, and took off in a madman's water sprint towards the sound. He could not imagine there were too many people this time of night getting dropped off and left to their death. Charlie was definitely the one he'd heard. He had heard him curse more than once when they worked on the boat together, and he could sew together a line of curse words like an artist, especially when someone had fucked something up. When it came to cursing like a sailor, they might have come up with that expression because of Charlie.

The slapping of water was growing louder by the second and was enticing Tim to swim even faster. He just hoped that he was not too late to help his good friend. He was glad that Jim had not leaped off the boat because sitting and waiting worrying would not have been his ideal choice. Charlie was doing his best; still trying to kick but continually forgetting with the extra weight on his legs it wasn't doing a hell of a lot to help him. He was trying to remain calm floating on his back and not in the least bit letting up cursing like a sailor. Charlie had basically concluded that unless some help came from somewhere very soon, he'd be dead in a very short time. He knew, even with him being in shape, he could only do this for so long, before a cramp or God knows what, maybe even just fatigue kicked in, and he'd go down, and never come back up again.

Charlie wasn't quite sure if he was going delusional or not. He thought that it might be a possibility given the fact that he thought he was beginning to hear things. Charlie didn't know a lot about the different ways to die that weren't from being choked out, breaking a neck, or using a good old-fashioned handgun or rifle, etc., and sending a piece of lead or full metal jacket in military cases straight into someone's head. He did know though that if you were lucky enough to meet your fate by drowning that it was supposedly one of the worst ways possible to die.

The last thing that he wanted to do as his body would begin slowing down and not working would be to still have some life left in him. It was not an amazingly appealing idea to think about taking his last breath as he slowly sank beneath the ocean's surface, watching the top of the water until everything around him was as black as night. Charlie began reciting the only prayer that he and his Uncle Joe had ever said at the small boat's dinner table.

He did not know if it would help, but he sure as shit didn't think it could hurt a thing. So long as God, he thought, didn't think that this was something he deserved which he was pretty sure he didn't. Charlie definitely went out of his way not to be a douchebag. When he had finished reciting it, he whispered, "God, Jesus, anyone, if you can help me, I might just end up being your biggest churchgoer ever. You just tell me what religion, and I will be there."

Tim had gotten his stride down legit by this point. A few questions that were going through his head were why in the fuck they couldn't have gotten just a little bit closer and then let him dive off to go see if Charlie was there. He knew that he had heard some gunshots off in the distance and quite frankly was really hoping that there even would be a boat coming back for him. When he had heard Charlie he yelled, "Well I hope that you're going to be down to praise a black Jesus because I'm here to save you."

Charlie's arms felt like he'd been in the gym for hours since his overly weighted feet weren't a helluva lot of help. He jumped, taking in a mouthful of water, swallowing, and then coughing until he puked it out, sending the disgusting taste of salt water out through his mouth and his nose, burning like a son of a bitch. Tim dry-heaved when he smelled and saw the puke water. He said, "Goddamnit. I was here to save you. I didn't sign up for swimming in your goddamn puke."

Charlie swam back a few feet out of his own mess and let Tim put a lifeguard hold, keeping the two of them up and safe without any issues. He had probably never been happier to see Tim in his life, although when he had thought he was going to get a second-morning greeting of having his ass kicked he had been pretty happy to see the guys then as well. Charlie said, "How in the fuck did you find me?"

"The iPhone signal."

"Yeah, so again how in the fuck did the two of you find me? I know you're not that smart, and Jim well, duh."

"Really Ford, you're gonna bust my balls after I just swam mine off to find you in the middle of the fucking night?"

Charlie reached his hand back, patting Tim on the head. His bald head was pretty cool between the night air and the cool water. Charlie said, "No, I absolutely am not going to bust your balls. I've never been so goddamn happy in my whole fucking life to see you."

Tim laughed, "Stop petting my head, you weirdo. Oh, and I'd say between this and our truck getting blown up because of those dipshits at the docks almost killing us, you owe me big time."

"I owe you a hell of a lot more than one. Are you fucking kidding me? All I know is as soon as we get back to shore there's going to be some serious fuckery going on with going after Bruno and Lou and the other two dipshits."

"Amen to that, brother. Just hang out a minute, maybe feel free to try and kick your feet or do anything useful. If you don't think that maybe that is too much to ask out of you."

Charlie realized he was probably coming off like an absolute pussy but knew in his defense It wasn't entirely his fault. Charlie managed to get one of his legs up, not that Tim could really see it but said, "If you could see my leg, you would also see that there's a pretty decent amount of cement on it."

Tim, just like Jim, was always happy to bust a fellow soldier's balls especially when they belonged to one of his very best friends, Charlie Ford. Tim asked, "So why in the fuck do you have cement on your feet, genius? Don't you know that there's a reason people don't do that?"

"You know, I thought the same thing, Tim. During our boat ride, I never had the chance to ask Lou and Bruno why they had put my feet in a bucket of cement out in the middle of the ocean. It didn't seem like a good idea."

"You know I can't say that I'm too surprised that they did that. Is there a reason that they really really fucked up doing it though?"

"No, not one that I can think of that's intelligent. I think it was Lou that had gone to buy the cement, and unfortunately had not been intelligent enough to buy the quick-dry cement."

Tim laughed a little saying, "Wow that's definitely a special kind of stupid right there with their own reserved spot in hell for absolute idiots. Here I thought that Lou was the smart one out of the group."

Charlie nodded saying, "Well we can sure as hell hope so. I can't imagine those two have a ticket to the golden gates up above."

"If they do, I'm gonna add some sins to my lifestyle on a regular basis."

Tim patted Charlie on the chest, "Black Jesus doesn't care for talk like that, my son."

"You aren't going to hold me to that, are you? I mean, come on, I thought that I was going to die."

"You were going to die until I came and saved your ass. You best be kissing mine because of it."

There were lights in the distance. Charlie squinted, trying to think if they should dive or feel safe. From this distance, he didn't have a clue if he had friends or foes coming in his direction. Charlie reached behind his back pulling out a pistol. Charlie said, "Don't worry; it's empty."

"Why would I worry? I would feel better if you told me the magazine was full. What are you doing with an empty gun?"

"Well, it wasn't empty when I started, Tim."

"Since they had to chase after that boat, I'd think you needed to aim better."

"Yes, with my hands behind my back. That wasn't something I'd been trained on. But I guarantee you I'm going to have more hidden shit on my body to get me out of shit situations than you'll ever believe...once I find it. I'm quite thankful that I got that phone."

"Why don't we worry about your James Bond kit once we figure out if we are going to die or not?"

The two squinted; there was a spotlight that was the only real bright thing out here. Charlie hoped if they were going to die that it'd just be quick. He couldn't stand the thought of having to carry on any long conversations with those absolute idiots. The light grew brighter the closer it got until there was a circle around them that had to have been ten feet wide. Charlie whispered, "Hey, I'm really sorry that I got you guys into this, Tim. It wasn't supposed to go down like this. The good guys were supposed to win. I'm sorry that didn't happen."

A voice they recognized yelled, "Do you two want a little more time together? Tim, it looks like you are getting set up to give Charlie a reach around. Is that what you are thinking of? I mean Jesus, Ford, we come all the way down here, save your life a couple times and you don't have the decency to tug on Tim's third leg for a minute?"

Charlie, who'd been doing his damndest to just float with his cement-covered feet and legs, raised up a free hand. He happily knew that because they were such good friends that no one would be offended as Charlie raised his middle finger loud and proud for Jim and his comments. Johnney pulled the window open yelling, "What kind of weird shit are you guys talking about? Jesus Christ, for love of God, third leg? What in the goddamn hell's wrong with you guys?"

Jim reached down, taking Charlie's hand not quite noticing just at first that he had a few extra pounds on him. Jim said, "Maybe you need to cut back a little bit on everything, Charlie."

Charlie pulled himself the rest of the way up and that was when Jim saw his legs and the excess that he somehow had accrued. Johnney saw as well as Cliff saying, "I thought they only did stupid shit like that in the movies, damn it. Those guys really are that fucking stupid, aren't they?"

Charlie could only shrug. He assumed that they were definitely that stupid. Johnney didn't waste any time and went to the kitchen galley, getting as many pots as he could find filled up with water, sending Cliff out one at a time with each one. Johnney said, "Tell him to take this rag and dampen that shit as much as he can. I got a good feeling most of it came off when he was submerged. Some cement is a little bit more stubborn than the others. It really all just depends."

Cliff nodded, thinking that the next time some crazy shit was happening that he very well might just decide that he should just pass on doing any good deeds. He really didn't have anything against being a good person, but he'd be damned if he was gonna die for a complete stranger. He also could not say that he was overly excited about one guaranteed fact which was he was going to need to find a new job.

He was pretty sure no one here would be able to offer him any sort of gainful employment. Cliff knew that if they could that it probably wasn't going to be any job that he was interested in having. Cliff was super not excited to tell his girlfriend Chandra about his change in employment status. These guys definitely seemed like they might be the type to get into a hell of a lot of trouble. Way too goddamn often, he would guess. Cliff had never been one for trouble and quite frankly wasn't changing his ways now. When he headed back out, Charlie handed him the phone. He said, "Hey, I guess I owe you…you know, my life. I don't know if I broke your phone or not."

"Dude, I live in Florida and love the beach. That case is waterproof. I don't think you'd have been able to unlock it, but that wasn't really the point of putting it on the boat."

Charlie spent the better part of a half-hour, as they took the boat back to his dock, getting as absolutely much of the cement off his legs as he could, while attempting to save the skin which it was attached to. He wasn't quite sure what the chemical damage would do to skin with that much cement, mostly of course because he'd never had that much cement on him. He couldn't really see his legs all that great in the darkness, but he could definitely tell there were some sensitivity issues going on. By the time he had finished, Charlie figured some burn medicine and lotion might not hurt a single thing. The only thing that kept him from riding the entire way home in as much spite as possible was when they'd explained what they'd done to Lou and Bruno's boat, leaving them stranded.

When they got back to shore, Johnney stuck his head out asking, "What are you boys gonna do now?"

Charlie replied, "I think it's about time to go have a conversation with Nydegger Esquire about his business practices. Hopefully, he's got some great answers or there might be one less lawyer in the world."

Johnney nodded saying, "Well if you get in a tight spot, you do me a favor will ya and don't call me. I'm too old for this shit and I'm going to go home and go to bed. I'm fucking tired. I don't need excitement like this in my life. Chances are, it is gonna make my brain or heart go and explode."

Chapter 3

Lou and Bruno knew that they needed to get out of there and they needed to do it quickly. Neither of them felt like they were an accomplished swimmer and did not have a lot of self-interest in attempting to see how long they would be able to keep afloat. Bruno kept shoving the phone at Lou who was dead set shaking his head no that he was not going to be the one to make the call.

Bruno was getting more upset by the second about him saying no to doing this, but in the end, Lou had more than stood up for himself, and just about the only reason Bruno had taken the excuse or the reasoning why he shouldn't have to call him had been a very simple fact. That simple fact was that he had had the tip of his tongue bitten off when Charlie had cracked him in the head and quite frankly Lou was next to impossible to be heard or maybe not to be heard but to be understood. Given where they were needed to be specific, having someone who couldn't use words with 's' in them didn't seem the wisest.

Bruno took the phone, hating everything about it and hitting the speed dial for Nydegger. It pained him to call the boss. He waited, and in less than a minute Nydegger had answered the phone in more of a question than anything else, saying or asking, "Bruno?"

"Yeah boss, we had a bit of an issue. We need a ride, like now!"

"I can send Sid and Minty. Where are you, and how far of a drive is it?"

"About a half-hour...by boat."

"So, you accomplished what you said that you would do? So, you aren't calling with only bad news?"

"We tried to do it. We had a few things that didn't end up going our way."

"Such as?"

"Sir, we really need a ride. We aren't so much sitting out here in a broken-down boat, as you might say we are in a sinking boat filled with bullet holes."

"How is it going to look, if I don't punish you two for fucking up?"

"Well, Sid and Minty must have fucked up too, because if they hadn't come to get him in his own boat then we would have not had a very difficult job of getting him taken care of."

Nydegger asked more rhetorically than anything saying, "Is there a reason for the love of God that I only have idiots working for me? Should I be asking who contracted me for more money so I can hire more intelligent help?"

Bruno was pretty sure he wasn't supposed to answer a question with a question but said, "I don't know if you should ask for more money when you keep not getting the job done."

Nydegger said, "Send me your coordinates now. I'll try and get those two out there to get you in time. If you drown, just remember you probably deserved it."

"You're too kind, Mr. Nydegger."

"Yes, I know. Do you think that I have anything to worry about, Bruno?"

"Yeah, I'd say you have a pretty goddamn big problem coming your way with about a half-hour lead on us."

"Great, that's exactly what I needed to hear. Do me a favor: once you get back to land, can you guys just stay low for a little bit, please? I think I'm going to take a short sabbatical for a week or two, and hopefully, things will blow over. How long can they stay mad for?"

His answer came with the click of a hammer from a handgun. One of the two worst sounds ever; the second was the pump action on a shotgun, which is what the next sound was. Nydegger was not knowledgeable about guns whatsoever. But that was definitely a sound much like the racking of a shotgun that he knew very well.

Nydegger knew better than to play the hero or the tough guy. Right now, he was all by his lonesome. There wasn't anyone here but himself and maybe a cleaning lady...one who he couldn't say what her name was and would be quite surprised if she cared that one, he got shot, and two that she wouldn't just leave and mind her own business...something he knew could keep you alive. He raised his hands slowly.

Jim and Tim both looked at each other. Neither of them had asked him to do a thing. Jim said, "You can put your hands down, or keep them up."

He said, "Hey, I need to make a very important call. It is a matter of life or death though. Please, if you don't mind, I'll just be a min..."

Charlie hit him in the back of his head with the muzzle of the gun, "If that was an SOS call from Bruno and Lou, let them float."

"You are going to be on their kill list, Mr. Ford."

"Really, that is terrifying, Nydegger. I mean two guys who kidnapped me, took me on a boat, used slow dry cement, and then cuffed my hands behind my back and still couldn't finish the job. Because that is a very scary thought; titillating, you might say."

Jim said, "Are we talking about boobs or the idiots that couldn't kill you?"

"Minus the boobs, it is the same thing, Jim, try to keep up."

Nydegger was going to say how this was a big misunderstanding. But he did not take Charlie as an idiot. He couldn't necessarily say the same about Jim, but all in all, he felt confident he might just shut up for a minute. Charlie took a hold of the back of his suit coat, pulling him in close saying, "Since you have been trying to kill me, you also had people kick the shit out of me, so much that I needed to call in reinforcements. So, why don't you tell me what in the fuck it is that you want? Oh, and once we dive into that conversation, we're also going to talk about you killing my only relative left that I had in the world."

Nydegger knew that what he was saying was the truth, or better, what he was going to say would be the truth. However, he did think that it wasn't going to do a hell of a lot of good because he had put in the order to have it done. Nydegger tried to say calmly, "I did not kill your Uncle Joe. I swear to god."

Charlie spun Nydegger around, lifting and slamming him down onto a glass table. The glass could not handle Mr. Nydegger Esquire's weight, and it shattered instantly, covering the back of his head with small cuts when he landed flat on the floor, hitting his head hard into it. Charlie knelt down, putting the handgun up next to his face replying, "I'm sure you didn't kill my Uncle Joe. It would have had to have taken quite a few of you. But I do think that you hired it out, and you either have a dirty fucking cop, or a stupid fucking cop working for you. Then you either had the guy at the meat locker falsify the information about Uncle Joe or you guys pumped him full of booze and then decided it was time to kill him. So, I would say right now is probably the ideal time for you, if you'd like to continue living, to start telling the truth.

Nydegger looked like he had deflated. He said, "I had nothing against your Uncle Joe. I swear he did legitimately come to me to have everything set up in his will to go to you."

"Is that what you do? Someone hires you to do a job, and then you do it. I can only assume you get paid and then kill them?"

"Look, Charlie, it wasn't me…"

Charlie cut him off by punching him in the face twice and said, "We've already determined that it wasn't you. So why don't you tell me who it was? I know that there's no chance you're the criminal mastermind. The cloth that you're cut from isn't worth shit. I've met hard men, and you sure as fuck aren't one."

"Look, I wasn't trying to say that I'm some criminal mastermind or badass with a gun or something. You might say that I'm an intermediary. I was the middleman, okay? Just relax, and for God's sake, please don't punch me in the face anymore."

Charlie looked at Tim and Jim, but neither of them knew anything more about what was happening down here than he did. Charlie asked, "So you've got the detectives? I assume that's right?"

"I've got a detective, and he works cheap."

"Yeah, I kind of figured that."

"These people were put into my care. I didn't ask for any of this.

Someone approached me and asked how much for my services and then from there I was supposed to be in charge of everything.”

“Could you just get to the point of who I'm going to go kill?”

Nydegger laughed a little at this, not meaning any offense, and actually hadn't meant to laugh in the first place but looked as guilty as he felt about everything that had happened. He didn't think that sending Charlie on a guaranteed mission of death was going to help him all that much either.

Tim took the break in silence as an insult that he needed a little additional persuasion to talk. He took Nydegger by the front of his shirt, bringing up a fist that looked like a football and Nydegger closed his eyes yelling quickly, “It's Fratto, it's different! Don't hit me, God dammit. Don't hit me again! Fratto ordered it, not me.”

Charlie waited for him to open his eyes, and when he didn't, slapped him across the face yelling, “Open your fucking eyes, Nydegger, and I won't hit you.”

“You just did hit me!” Nydegger screamed.

“Oh, for God's sake. Okay, I won't punch you. How's that? I can't guarantee that I'm going to take bitch slapping off the table with someone like you.”

Nydegger held up a nonthreatening hand flat nodding, thinking so long as it wasn't a plethora of bitch slaps that it was something he could probably put up with. Nydegger said, "It is Fratto, okay?"

"You keep saying the same thing. Look, I've already had a conversation with him since I've been in town. His guys seem to be a hell of a lot more effective than your so-called crew. You think he's going to appreciate it if you're spreading rumors about him and what you think he's doing?"

"I said, Fratto. I didn't say which one."

Charlie had had a very long day which was turning into a long night which appeared to look like it might be woven into the next morning. He said, "There are multiple Frattos down here?"

"Well yeah, but that's not what I mean. Look, his kid wanted to take over part of his dad's business. His dad's had him doing collections for as long as I've been around. Junior thinks that he's set up to do bigger things in life. You know that he's perfectly capable of committing larger crimes."

"Well, we can always pray that our kids would follow in our footsteps, right?"

Nydegger wasn't sure if he should laugh or not because he had been on the opposite end of an interrogation like this before, and typically, once you got someone relaxed, that was when you would punch them in the face again and again. Not himself, of course, he thought, but somebody much bigger, like Bruno or Lou if he had his brass knuckles on him to do the dirty work. Charlie started putting things together pretty quickly at that point. Charlie asked, "So, his kid Junior is who hired you and got you some idiotic thugs to work with you along with the dirty cop?"

"Yeah, the guy down at the morgue didn't have anything to do with it. Detective Lindvall went and changed the documents after he had completed his initial findings. He messed them up so that it looked like your uncle had been drinking like a fish. We didn't know anything about him quitting drinking, so we thought it was pretty perfect, to be honest. The guy in the morgue went back and saw what had happened. Lindvall tried getting him to play ball. He didn't see the point in doing that and therefore he needed to be taken care of."

"And what happened to my Uncle Joe? If he just wanted to take over the business, then why wouldn't he just try and keep him alive?"

"Killing him was never the intention. The group of four bumbling idiots used to be five. They went to try and talk to your uncle, making sure before they made any big plays that he would be on board with the idea of taking over things. They also wanted to make sure loyalty wouldn't be an issue as he'd been working for Fratto for a hell of a long time."

"So, Uncle Joe killed one of them, I'm assuming, probably when he said to go stick it up their fucking asses?"

"Yes, actually, it's pretty damn close to that, to be honest. Before they could really try and apply any muscle, he'd brought a knife out of nowhere and slit the man's neck, left to right an inch deep. With the size of the boat inside, they couldn't even make it up to him until he was done, and the man was bleeding like a stuck pig."

"Good, it is too bad he didn't have time to take a few more. Would have ridden the world of some real pieces of shit."

"Well, there's always another one to take their places."

"So why did they want to buy my boat so badly?"

"The cargo compartments are custom-built The GPS if we could hack it, is programmed to get the specific routes. He came up with all that on his own, through lots of trials. Your uncle was a helluva seaman."

"I'm assuming if Junior is still alive, that Fratto doesn't know any of this?"

"You could say that pretty confidently, Charlie. Unfortunately, if anyone's gonna kill that kid, it's probably going to be his own father. He does not put up with any disrespect. So, if someone, maybe you or your two giants here, were to tell him what was happening, then he might be prone to thanking you and taking care of everything else."

"So, what would happen if I went and took care of things?"

"That's actually the easiest question you've asked so far. Unlike Bruno and Lou, Mr. Fratto doesn't do things twice. He does them once. He makes it calculated. He's precise and he doesn't fuck up. But if you went and did what he might think is his job and right, then you'll probably fall on a list you'd rather not be on, quite quickly."

Charlie really wished that he would have had the opportunity to do this on his own. But if they were going to stay down here then he needed to have some people still on his good side. Charlie replied, "Would it be safe to say that tonight is your last night running a criminal empire or being the middleman for one?"

"Definitely, most definitely. You can trust me."

"Oh, for sure, a crooked lawyer who had Charlie's uncle killed, and then tried to blow us up. Not to forget, you took Charlie out on a boat with two idiots not smart enough to let cement set before letting Charlie get in the water. That's definitely who I want to trust," Jim said.

Charlie pulled Nydegger up to a sitting position, noticing he had never dropped his phone, and as a result of that he also looked to have dialed a phone number while he was waiting for this to end one way or another. Jim noticed the light from it and gripped him by the wrist, squeezing until he let go. The phone dropped to the ground sending the glass flying in different directions and Nydegger said in a quivering tone, "I had already called them as soon as you showed up. I didn't know that you were here and were going to let me live. I didn't know. I didn't know!"

Charlie was definitely thinking if he did not have a gun registered to himself on him right now that he would have happily shot Nydegger twice in the face. He was thinking that he did have Lou's gun but didn't want to have to worry about gun residue and any type of blowback from the gun coming back to bite him in the ass.

Charlie leaned down saying, "If I were you, it might be a very wise idea if I don't see you again for a while. I can only imagine the brownie points that I'll accrue when I get to talk to Fratto."

Nydegger was feeling a little bit more confident at the moment, even though he still had a gun pointed at the rear of his head. He could feel blood coming from multiple cuts, some larger than others on his head. Nydegger said, "I'm an upstanding citizen in the Keys community, Charlie. I'm not going anywhere. I have a feeling you're not going to be going anywhere either once you go outside."

"Well, I was hoping that it would be your detective out there. I have a feeling I've got something saved up in the cloud that he might be interested in seeing before he decides what he wants to do with us. Oh, and you know, your complete confession as well."

"You fucking idiot. I would never repeat that again."

Jim held out his phone saying, "Well, then it's a good thing that I have a really good recording system on this phone. I mean, really good. You should see this video a Jamaican chick and I made. Oh my god, if I wanted kids and a wife, I'd marry her. No worries though, I saved it up in the cloud already."

Nydegger sunk his head back down onto the ground, not really caring about the new wounds that he was self-inflicting. He knew that there was a strong chance shit was going to get way worse before it got better. The three got up, looking out front, seeing a sports utility vehicle that had no lights on the top of it, but it did have state plates. To boot, it also had a siren light blinking on the inside. When they went out, they went out slowly after unloading the guns, taking them apart, and walking outside. They didn't leave any question about the fact they were not presenting a danger to anyone.

Detective Lindvall yelled, "You three fucks stop moving now, otherwise I'm going to blow a hole right through your fucking heads. Put everything on the ground now!"

They stopped, not giving him any valid reason to shoot them. Lindvall must have felt like showing his authority and yelled again, "I said to put everything down now!"

Jim said, "Very hard to do that, sir. See this is a cell phone, and currently, you're live on the Florida Keys Facebook Page. It would be really awkward if you shot three unarmed men, especially with one of them being as handsome as I am."

The detective deflated a little bit. Lindvall wasn't big on social media and was wondering if they actually had a page. He knew that he could get away with murder, quite literally in some cases, but video evidence and cops did not go hand in hand, especially nowadays. People would judge him by the video and not care about what was behind it.

Charlie smiled, saying, "Detective Lindvall, you look like someone just shot your puppy, or is it that we shot your chance of shooting us?"

Lindvall looked around the parking lot, and he didn't really have any answers to be had. He couldn't think of any intelligent reason why he could get out of a conviction by shooting three men that had their arms up. The redheaded fellow in the back seemed to have a pretty damn good angle too. He had the reverse angle going on it, so Lindvall knew he was surely in frame. Lindvall said, "Good work, guys. Do you have permits for those weapons?"

Tim asked, "You mean these disassembled weapons? Ones that would probably take 10 or 15 minutes to put back together before they would be functional?"

Lindvall knew the things he had at the moment seemed to be running low in regards to reasons to detain these three. Jim said, "Is there actually a reason that you're detaining us, detective?"

Lindvall knew with a corroborated statement from Nydegger that he could take them to jail. But the more he thought about it, he realized Nydegger just wanted most likely a reason for these guys to get the fuck out of his office. Lindvall had not enjoyed working with Nydegger whatsoever. It had not been a request of his to get farmed out. But he knew that there were certain people in the Keys who you did not say no to, or in this case, it was someone whom eventually you would not say no to.

Lindvall put his gun away, walking up, patting the three of them down, and saying, "You best get your shit figured out in this town, Charlie, or you're going to end up having some serious issues here. I don't think that this is the kind of shit you want to start in town. You with the camera; you can turn it off. You guys will be free to go once I'm done talking. So, turn the damn thing off."

Jim said, "How about I just go stand over there with it on? But then I won't get to hear your secret whispers. How does that sound?"

"It sounds like you're gonna be a pain in the ass too. You realize there's hundreds of miles of coastline in America, right? Plenty of places that you three could go to live that isn't here."

Charlie smiled while waiting for Jim to go wait with Tim. Charlie said, "I'm going to pull my phone out of my pocket. I'm going to show you something, and then you're going to leave us alone."

"Oh really? That's adorable. What kind of leverage do you have or that you think you have that would make me do anything that I don't want to do?"

Charlie opened up the phone going to a saved folder and said, "Before you get any ideas, this is in the cloud too. Just like Nydegger's confession, the one you probably heard that included dirty cops from the Florida Keys Police Department, aka you. But this one is especially good for you. Do you remember the guy that worked at the morgue that I'm assuming did not like how you played ball? Like how you changed his report to make it look like my Uncle Joe had drank himself to death. Well, believe it or not, I wasn't the biggest fan of that. So, after you and I had had a conversation, I decided it would be a good idea to go have a conversation of my own with him. When I went to their house, I found the two of them hanging, each by their own noose for what I had to assume would have been at least two days longer than I had been in the Keys. Hell, you can't even blame it on Joe. He was dead too."

"You went into a crime scene?"

"It wasn't a crime scene. No one knew that they were dead. I didn't know that until I got there."

"Well, it would have been a crime scene had you waited."

"Waited for what, hell to freeze over?"

"Look, smartass, you can't just go around town doing whatever you want. There's rules you need to follow, and people you need to talk to first."

Charlie showed him the phone. The picture, which was time-stamped, as well as clear as day showed the two hanging with nothing in front of them was pretty evident. Charlie said, "You know, I'd have to guess that these two might not have died by being hung. I think there's a very strong chance that it was the aftermath of strangulation, someone who thought they could make it look legit of course did it. It had to be an idiot. Was it one of yours?"

"Watch it, Charlie, you are getting pretty deep down here, son…"

"Yeah, I'm anything but your fucking son. Oh, and your dipshits, well…they fucked up when they didn't put chairs under the people. Each one of them was what, five-five? They had vaulted ceilings for God's sakes. How in the fuck would they get up to tie off the rope? Let alone get the noose and then hang themselves by it?"

"Look, it was taken as a suicide".

Charlie smiled saying, "Well, would your name be at the bottom of the report for this? Seeing as there's not a hell of a lot of people who are detectives where you are at."

"Are you sure you want to go there? I mean the three of you are positive, you know that this is the kind of relationship that you want to have?"

Charlie smiled, saying, "I'm not saying anything. I'm just saying your names on those reports and this picture sure lends itself to not being anything that corroborates what you've got in your report if I had to guess."

"I've dealt with smarter guys than you. Trust me, this would just be a few unpleasant days for me. But unlike you, I would and will survive this."

"So, if I sent this to 'The Reporter' newspaper you wouldn't have any issues. You know, if a detective from an honest precinct started looking into you, and your bank accounts, both foreign and domestic of course. Maybe then they start looking at some of your old cases and questioning people. I'm sure you have a few that were legit back in the day, but I can't imagine that you lend yourself to anything that doesn't help you in the long run. Would that be impolite of me to say or would the number of your skeletons falling out of the closet make it hard to shut the door?"

Charlie walked back to his friends, trying to gauge where this was gonna go. Lindvall said, "Well, I guess one other question is going to be if you think threatening an officer is actually legal. It might very well be a fact that you could definitely stir up some shit in my life. But I can get you guys locked up for at least a few hours, and I'll figure out what I'm going to do next."

Tim leaned over whispering, "I do not want to go to this motherfucker's jail. Do you have any bright ideas?"

Charlie absolutely didn't and said it again advising, "Just

remember what I said about having backups of this. Anything happens to me…"

"Yeah, I'm sure that I already know. You are going to have something set up so people will know that something horrific happened to you and your friends. Is that about the gist of it?"

Charlie was nodding his head when Lindvall asked, "And if the three of you are in jail, who's gonna send it out?"

Charlie said, "Don't worry about it. I'm a very technical guy, I have it set up with a good authority that it'll go out automatically if I don't log into the email every so often and change the date to send it. So, you might want to make sure that you don't keep us in there for too long. I've still got plenty of things going on in life that I need to figure out."

Lindvall escorted the three to the back of his car taking the phones from Jim and Tim as well as Charlie's and threw them in the front seat of the SUV and put them in the back; it was not a spot meant for three people. If Charlie had been the size of Tim and Jim, it'd have been near impossible to close the door. Lindvall was outside trying to talk with Nydegger who was shaking his head, absolutely hell-bent on not giving up any useful information.

Lindvall could be heard yelling, "The next time, if you're not going to fucking help, don't call me for help. Now I've got an entirely brand-new list of shit that I have to fucking deal with. I don't think that you appreciate the situation that you are putting me in."

Nydegger pulled out a white envelope, handing it over and trying not to look like he was going to shit his pants. Lindvall, to no surprise to anyone, accepted it. Nydegger turned around, taking his bloody self back into his own building to clean up, and if Charlie had to make an assumption, he would more than likely be very interested in a very stiff drink as he pondered if he'd live or die.

Chapter 4

Tim looked over at Charlie and Jim saying, "You know, call me crazy, but when I thought you needed help, I wasn't necessarily anticipating needing to post bail. I mean, it isn't anything personal, but basically, anything over the amount of money in my pocket currently is more than I probably have. I don't know too many good bail bondsmen down here; I mean maybe I could get lucky and there could be a lonely lady running it that might like some personal attention."

Jim laughed saying, "Really, you haven't even gotten to jail yet and you're already ready to whore yourself for sex. Good lord, what in the hell, that's pretty fucked up. I mean you aren't even that good-looking."

Tim was really only half-joking. He really didn't like the idea of going to jail at all. One of the things he had always prided himself on was not being an idiot, which also meant not making stupid decisions that would land his ass in jail. Anything he did he knew was legal. So, the last few days had been somewhat stressful on him.

Charlie said, "Don't worry about it. I happen to have a boat worth a pretty good amount of money. I don't really think they have us on a hell of a lot. My best guess here is he's buying himself some time to figure out what the hell he's going to do. I wouldn't imagine the judge is going to be too overly happy about the fact that he's probably having his time wasted by a detective. We can only hope that at some point in the rungs of the ladder of the law someone here is not a criminal."

Jim said, "I don't know, three meals with a nice, padded bed. Hell, it might feel like we're back on the ship, you know, except for maybe the bars."

Charlie said, "I haven't been out long enough to miss it, or to want to go back. I could imagine one day wanting to, but it's only been a few."

Lindvall came back to his SUV, looking in the back at the three, thinking it would probably be easier to just drown them than have to deal with them on an ongoing basis. Lindvall said, "So the three of you are going to jail for the night at least. Nydegger wouldn't say anything, but I still have a sinking suspicion that he wasn't bloody when you walked in there. So, I'm gonna hold you for at least 24 hours to try and get things figured out, or longer."

Jim leaned forward, putting his cuffed hands on the back of Lindvall's seat saying, "Is it because I'm black?"

Lindvall looked at Jim smiling. His pale white skin and red hair made it all that much more annoying. Tim, sitting next to him, didn't even want to open that bag of chips; he just shook his head. Lindvall said, "Let me just read you your rights to make sure that there are no questions about anything just on the off chance that they end up deciding you are actually guilty of something."

Chapter 5

By the time Lindvall had pulled into the booking station side of the jail, he was pretty sure that Jim might have been the least favorite person he'd ever had to arrest before. When he had asked him if he ever shut up, Tim and Charlie had said no without the need for a second's hesitation. Charlie had said, "You know if you let us go, we can take Jim with us. Then you wouldn't have to listen to him anymore."

"Well, as tempting as that is, I'm still pretty sure you're guilty of a few crimes. So, I'll just do my damnedest not to pay any attention to him. Which, once you guys are back in cells, probably should not be an issue. I mean it is a perk of the job to drop off the piece of shits and be done with them until trial."

The front desk sergeant recognized Charlie saying, "You back so soon? If she's whooping your ass, all you gotta do is press charges."

"It wasn't necessarily by choice."

"What did you do?" He questioned.

"You know that's a really funny question, and I have a great story. But I'm gonna pick the right to remain silent as part of my Miranda rights. I mean if that's okay with you?"

"Oh, come on, I wouldn't tell on you. You can trust me."

"Yeah, as much as I can trust a hooker that said I don't need to wrap it up. You know because herpes is forever."

The three went through a quick booking process, and within a half-hour, they were all sitting waiting to be put in their cells. They had gotten some nice flip-flops in exchange for their leather shoes and boots. They had taken away belts, chains, and all other personal belongings the three of them had in their pockets. Charlie had half expected to be asked to bend over and spread cheeks but thank God that had not been the case.

When they walked back into the jail housing unit of the police station, they were kind of surprised at how many people were in the jail in the first place. Charlie said, "Wow, these guys must be really busy arresting people that didn't do anything. We never had this many people in our jail on the ship. Of course, it's a hell of a lot harder to fill up the jail when you're arresting guilty people that you've had to actually catch in the middle of a crime. I mean, Jesus, if we could just go and arrest every Tom, Dick, and Harry then shit, our job would have been a hell of a lot easier and probably would have all gotten raises regularly for keeping the ship so safe."

The cell guard didn't say anything; he just walked Charlie back. He was gonna get paid regardless of what these guys thought. He'd heard every single excuse from every person he'd walked back; some drunk, others high, and even more bloodied from fights and other bad things people shouldn't have done.

Charlie got put in the cell at the end, noticing the line of bars went all the way down to the end of the building. They had seven cells and the jailer put Charlie in cell G. He noticed he was not alone, even though there'd have been plenty of space to put everyone. The two guys in there did not fill him with a hell of a lot of confidence about how things might transpire going forward. Charlie watched as Jim and Tim each got put in separate cells as well. Both of them appeared to have cellmates already waiting for them. The jailer made sure all the gates to the cells were locked and said, "Now I don't want any trouble out of any of you tonight."

Charlie said, "When do we get to make our phone call?"

The jailer laughed at this, asking, "Who did you want to call, your lawyer? I have a feeling that you probably are not going..."

Charlie cut him off and said, "Well, luckily for me I actually had another phone number I needed to call. But, if you don't think that I deserve my constitutional right then just let me know. I'm sure I could find a few Florida Key lawyers with a hard-on for the criminal justice system down here. Probably someone that would work pro bono, so long as they end up getting a cut of the settlement check. I mean, I don't know, what do you think we could get guys, a million, million and a half...each? We could probably get enough to just be bums down here for as long as we want to. Would that be some shit?"

The jailer apparently was aware that two things must not be

lacking in the Florida Keys. The first seemed to be lawyers, and the second he assumed was the need for suing dirty cops who did stupid shit. The jailer didn't know Charlie, but he looked at the paperwork as he stood there debating his decision, and apparently, something about him being a former Naval police officer probably had leaped off the page and bitch slapped him in the face. The jailer was really hoping that Lindvall wasn't screwing him over, asking to make sure they got the special Keys jail treatment. The jailer hesitantly said, "I'll take the three of you to make your phone calls, one at a time."

Charlie looked at the other two saying, "Just make sure you call the meanest lawyers the two of you know, and remember we've got collateral."

Tim looked at him as he was walking from the back of the jail cells where he'd been put forward past them and said, "Is there a reason that you're not going to call the best piece of shit, meanest bulldog of a lawyer you can? I mean, except for Nydegger, Esquire, of course."

"Yes, but I don't think that I would like to tell you who I want to call directly in front of you know who," Charlie said, putting a hand up and pointing to the officer.

The guard let out an overly dramatic sigh. It would seem to Charlie that not really any of them seemed to be horrifically popular in the community of the Florida Keys, or at least in the police department so far. Charlie was pretty sure that he was easily and quickly turning into Leslie's, maybe not Mark's favorite customer, at her diner. However, he had been a police officer in the Navy, so he was very used to lots of people not liking him.

The guard pointed to the directions that showed how to make a call. Charlie was impressed that they had actually been able to fit so many different languages telling the so-called criminal what exactly they had to do so they would be able to make their one free phone call. Once the guy was gone, Charlie looked, around bending down grabbing a piece of paper that Fratto had given Charlie when they talked. Charlie was glad he was not a nether regions sweater and took a quick look, punching in the number, glad he hadn't lost it because what he thought he had memorized had not been the case. Charlie waited impatiently, getting more nervous by the second that he wasn't going to answer and didn't like the prospect of something already happening to Fratto while they were in jail.

The phone finally picked up; a voice that did not seem excited to talk answered. Charlie had to assume this phone number was strictly meant for calls that were not going to be well received. Charlie knew that wasting people's time was never taken with a grain of salt. Typically, he learned, especially from his time, which was ample, in the military, that people who were working for a living and were the ones being contacted didn't want to waste their time. For the most part, what he'd learned was that the lower you were on the military totem pole, the faster you should try to get right to the point and not fuck around. That was about the absolute last thing anyone ever wanted. So, Charlie got right to the point. Charlie said, "Mr. Fratto, this is Charlie Ford."

Charlie waited for a second, not quite sure if he should talk again or wait to be acknowledged. Fratto finally said, "You're the only one with this number, kid."

Charlie had not thought he was important enough to warrant having what he knew they call it in the biz: a burner phone dedicated to him. Charlie couldn't help himself saying, "Really?"

"If I give someone my word that I'm going to take care of them, That's exactly what I do, kid. I know that you're calling from the Keys jail. Do you need a lawyer sent your way?"

"No…well yes, I do actually. But sir, that isn't why I'm calling."

"I'll get someone headed your way very soon. He's a real fucking shark, really hates cops."

"That would be great, but I'm calling for you."

"Yeah, and you got me."

Charlie was growing a little frustrated, Fratto wasn't being rude, but for someone who was in charge of everything down here, he sure as hell didn't seem like he was on the path to figuring out what he was talking about. At least quickly. Charlie figured he needed to hurry this along before the call ended.

Charlie said, "We went to Nydegger Esquire's office, and he confessed to having Uncle Joe killed. Well, not to having him killed, but to entice him to work for him. Joe said no of course, and things got bad."

"Really? I wouldn't think that spineless prick would have the balls to hire a hit out on someone working for me."

"It isn't so much that he has the balls, sir. It's that he thinks, or at least this is what I think, that he is going to feel like he has some clout in the city. See, he thinks there's going to be a new boss in town. He wants to be on their favorable side."

"No shit?"

"Yes sir. We just learned about it tonight. Quite frankly, you were going to be my first call, but we got arrested before I could do anything. So, my shitty day is just getting more and more...well, shitty."

"Sounds like it. So, who's the idiot that thinks he's got to take over the city?"

Charlie responded, "Fratto..."

"I'm already running the city, kid."

"No, it's Fratto, Fratto Junior, you know, your son. Apparently, he thinks it's his time to step up and for you to step down."

Fratto could be heard sighing saying, "What a fucking idiot. That's just fantastic. Do you know how much shit I'm going to get in with his goddamn mother when I have to deliver this news? You realize this is the reason why men ask for blowjobs right? Rarely does one come back twenty-five years later to bite you in the ass. Obviously, so long as it was consensual."

"Yes, I don't have kids, and no offense sir, but your kid isn't making it seem like having one is going to make life any easier for anyone."

"Yeah, amen to that. You hang tight. Call me back once my lawyer gets you out of jail. You got it?"

"I do, but one small favor, sir, please. Can you make sure that whoever you get for us knows my friends Tim and Jim were put in jail at the exact same time as myself? They'll also need representation to get out of there."

"Jim, Tim, and Charlie. I got it. Anyone else you've made friends with in jail that you'd like to get out?"

"No sir, I'm pretty sure the only other people that are in jail at the moment have been put in here purposely to beat us until we are either beaten to a bloody pulp or dead."

"Try not to let that happen, not much my lawyer can do if the three of you are dead."

"I plan on staying alive if I've got a choice, sir."

"You do that. I need to let you go though. I think there are some wheels in motion...if you know what I mean," he said whispering lightly.

Charlie got the point, that shit must have been close...damn close to hitting the fan. Charlie said, "Stay safe, sir. Good luck with everything."

"You, too. Thanks, kid, I appreciate the info, I don't forget someone doing a solid for me."

Chapter 6

Fratto put down the cell phone. He could see lights flashing in the driver's rear-view and side mirrors. They weren't somewhere that was busy this late into the night. He knew that something was awry and unfortunately was pretty fucking sure he knew what it was. When Fratto looked he could see there was no shortage of the cars following him, being what looked like blacked-out SUVs coming and going so fast. He said, "Keene, I'm gonna need you to get your ass moving. I think we've got some people on our ass."

He looked in his rear-view, seeing there definitely was someone coming after them. Keene put his foot down and the car used the muscle it had a plethora of to accelerate away...at least for a minute. Fratto was looking out the back of the window. They hit a bump at the same time that he figured out that everyone on his payroll might not be on his side. To put it lightly, he was absolutely not a hundred percent confident in all his people being faithful. When he hit the bump, he bounced off the side of the seat just as the glass shattered in the rear window.

He ducked but took it wrong. It wasn't like he thought. When the second bullet came it blew out the side of the seat next to him. Fratto already knew what he was going to see when he turned around. Keene was firing and trying to drive at top speeds. Fratto shook his head. He'd had the guy for at least six months driving for him and had been pretty happy with him so far...of course, he definitely felt differently right now. One other thing he questioned strongly was who else on his crew had been bought off.

Fratto was getting more pissed by the second. He dived towards the floor, flipping up a seat. Keene crushed the brake firing off a few shots blindly over his shoulder. The car slid to a stop, fishtailing as it did, slamming the ass off a few garbage cans parked along the side of the street. Fratto rolled forward, not able to get to his gun. Keene punched the gas again very much wanting to keep Fratto off balance. He knew what Fratto thought about backstabbers. It was either going to be him or Fratto and if he had his choice it wasn't going to be him. Keene took off again, hoping to keep the old man off-balance, but it was too late, way too damn late. Fratto was frothing at the mouth; he couldn't be more livid. Fratto came up quickly, knocking his arm to the side so he wasn't going to get shot out of luck.

Fratto could have reached down and got the gun now, but that was going to not make him feel nearly as well as what he wanted to do. Fratto took the seat belt, pulling the extra slack out, and quickly wrapped it around Keene's neck. Keene tried to put a hand up next to it, but he was still trying to drive at the same time. He was bouncing off of everything that could be hit in the alley. Fratto and Keene both wanted to live, but one thing Fratto had that Keene didn't was rage, rage he was going to abso-fucking-lutely use right now, to kill Keene and to stay alive. Fratto used all of his weight to pull backward. The car began to slow down, and Keene was fighting less by the second. Fratto sat up, barely able to see his face. The pain Keene was feeling wasn't making him feel bad at all. Unfortunately, this wasn't Fratto's first rodeo, and he knew two important things, one, it wasn't quick when it came to strangling. It could take five to ten minutes or more. The second, he knew that there were more people behind him that were probably much better with a gun.

Keene, in a last-ditch effort, slammed on the brakes one more time. Keene pulled, with everything he had, forward until Fratto finally lost his grip. Keene turned around after putting the car in park, coming up on the bench seat, and turning around. He had both hands holding a pistol. Fratto was lying on the seat. Keene's strangled bloodshot eyes grew as large as saucers when he saw Fratto lying on his back.

Unlike Bruno, Fratto didn't believe in wasting money on pimping out guns to look like they had come from the Mexican drug cartel or a movie. No, Fratto had come up as a child starting with nothing and worked his way up, making calculated and intelligent decisions, keeping his money where he wanted it...in his pocket. Unlike the younger kids working for him that all had Glocks and any other fancy thing, Fratto had figured out what he wanted and stuck with it. He was aiming straight on with a Colt 1911 forty-five-caliber. He fired off two shots, each drilling into Keene's skull. His head snapped back violently from the gun's power. His brains and skull spread all over the back of the windshield. Keene slumped forward over the seat. Fratto had a lovely view through Keene's newly acquired hole in his head.

One of the things that Fratto liked most about the 45 platform was that it did its job very well. The only reason he had taken a second shot was because he was thoroughly fucking pissed-off. He could understand people wanting to get up in the world, but his son doing it to him, and now a stupid ass driver trying to just take him out. There were rules, things you had to do, and he was damn aware that none of those avenues had been explored before this was happening.

The one thing he really wanted and demanded was having the loyalty of his people, and if they didn't it was inexcusable. He would make sure that after today he would slam down a fucking iron fist if he needed to and make goddamn sure that everyone understood who the boss was and who would be for a very long time. Fratto knew he would not be taking this car anywhere after the beating it'd taken from Keene.

He wasn't worried about shooting Keene. The second shot might have been questionable, but the shots were so close he wasn't sure anyone would even be able to tell there were two shots...at least anyone in a forensic job that wanted to live. If Keene had done his job and killed Fratto, then he wouldn't have lasted a day before being killed. It was always better to kill than to leave people open to ask stupid questions.

Fratto lifted up a seat, knowing that it was always better to have and not need than the alternative to be true. The part under the seat had a thumbprint recognition scan. He laid his thumb on it, allowing it to open and give him exactly what he needed.

Fratto knew that, like anyone in charge, he could very well need to take care of himself from time to time, and his hour was most fucking definitely here. He pulled out a Browning shotgun with a barrel that was the longest one you could purchase. But it had been outdone in length by the extended tube for inserting extra shotgun shells. It almost looked ridiculous, but he would take ridiculous and functional over not having enough shells and ending up dead. He had a small go-bag on the off chance he needed cash and couldn't use cards and a handful of burner phones. Fratto tucked everything in his pockets and got ready for his next move.

Fratto pulled back the shotgun's action, making sure there was one ready to go in the chamber. He peered out the partially shattered window, looking and seeing a blacked-out SUV. It apparently had gotten ahead of the others and got to be the unlucky bastards to arrive first. Fratto wasn't scared to die but also was in no hurry to meet his maker. He knew that unless God had one hell of a sense of humor that he would not be seeing the pearly gates. So, spending as much time on Earth as possible was absolutely his life goal. The SUV stopped right next to the door. A man that he didn't recognize got out not waiting for backups. He pulled Fratto's door open, assuming and yelling, "Keene, did you get him…Keene?"

Fratto was sitting on the floor with his elbow resting on the seat. He had his 12-gauge shouldered and the orange single sight bead resting square on this guy's chest. Fratto fired off a slug directly into the man, dead center. It sent him up off his feet and a foot back where he stumbled to his ass where he was dead before he hit the ground. Fratto didn't wait for the next participant to get up next to the car. He knew that the next guy might not be as stupid. Fratto slid his ass over until he could get out of the rear of the car. When he came out, Fratto had his gun already aimed and fired off a handful of slugs, tearing apart the front windshield of the SUV. Fratto walked around, making sure no one was left. He could tell by the lack of face the driver had he wouldn't be a problem. When Fratto opened the door, a man was cowering in his seat or to be more accurate where his legs would be if he wasn't cowering on the floor. It was yet another thug that he didn't recognize. He really had no qualms about killing them either way. If they were stupid enough to try and bring the heat to him, then Fratto would fucking charbroil everyone that got in his way.

The man whimpered, pleading for his life, "I'm sorry, I'm sorry. It wasn't supposed to go down like this! I don't want to work for this guy anyways. Let me work for you, I'll never let you down. I promise I promise!"

"You wouldn't make it as one of my guys."

"Why, I take orders?"

"Because one of my men wouldn't be on the floor in the first place. And of course, it wasn't supposed to go down this way, you fucking twat. You were supposed to kill me, I was supposed to die, and you guys thought you're gonna take over the Keys. Well, that isn't happening until it's over my dead fucking body, which sure as shit won't be because of you half-ass fucks, and it won't be tonight."

The man held up his hands screaming no as Fratto pulled the trigger sending a slug through both of the man's palms. It tore through them without bias, exploding in and out of his skull. Fratto didn't get turned stomachs, he cut his teeth doing the things that most others didn't want to. He made sure that his hierarchy got to a point where he was either going to be irreplaceable or it would be irrefutable that he should not be fucked with.

Fratto could feel a warm sensation in his chest. That feeling just like these guys could not have been more unwelcome at the moment. He felt around in his suit coat looking for his pills and when he found them realized he didn't have any water and wasn't a fan of dry-swallowing them. If he wasn't aging, he'd prefer not to take any drugs. Fratto looked around, seeing where he was, the businesses were not friendly to the Italians, but he knew he either needed to drive out of there or find a goddamn place to hole up.

His question on what he should do had quickly been decided for him. Fratto realized he didn't have the time needed to fuck around right now. The main reason for this was on account of even more SUVs who had been quite a bit luckier than their constituents and had not made it there quite as quickly.

Fratto went to the front of his car, opened the door, and grabbed Keene by the back of the neck, dragging him out of the driver's seat. Keene fell down on the concrete in an awkward pretzel-looking mess on the ground below. Fratto was capable of guilt, but never ever felt it at a time or a circumstance like this.

Fratto looked at the bloody windshield, not wanting to give any additional reason for the police to pull them over. He took Keene's water, knowing the first thing was first. Fratto took the top off and slammed a few drinks, getting some pills down for his heart, hoping his chest would feel better once he could enjoy a minute of peace without someone trying to murder him. He took the remainder of the bottle, squeezing and spraying it out like a geyser on the glass. If he couldn't see shit then taking the car wasn't going to do him a hell of a lot of good. The SUV was stuck behind and shot to shit in the front, which wasn't going to look great to anyone honest passing by while he was driving.

He hadn't driven himself in years. He looked at the futuristic dash panel in front of him remembering sitting behind a 1957 Chevy that had a lighter, a keyhole, and a knob for the radio. Which in his day had what was considered the fancy version with the memory buttons for what was considered programming back then. When he realized there wasn't a key slot, he could only assume the button in front of him was to start it and stop it. He hit the button, waiting for the engine to come to life.

But what he expected and got were two different things. An English accent came over the speakers saying, 'Thumbprint not recognized, thumbprint not recognized. Please try again.'

The fact that this was his car, but it was programmed to his driver's fingerprint felt more than just a little bit ignorant to him. Fratto got back out of the car pulling a knife and with zero hesitation picked up Keene's right hand and cut his thumb clean off with a Japanese knife someone he had had business dealings with had bestowed as a gift to him. Now the only thing that he was worried about was if there was a certain temperature that the finger had to be at. Regardless, Fratto was pretty sure that it wouldn't make a big difference given the simple fact that he had not had enough time to cool off yet.

Fratto crossed his fingers sticking the thumb up with his other hand and the supercharged V8 engine came to life. He revved it a few times before putting it in drive and punching the gas pedal down, making this elegant car which had a beast under the hood catapult them forward. Fratto smiled a little. He knew the electric cars were gaining much respect in the performance world but a V8 still fit to his liking just fine.

As soon as Fratto got out on an open street ran the windshield wipers, getting the busted glass off the front of the car, trying to look a little bit less conspicuous than he had a second ago. Once he got on a street that was crowded, he felt just a little bit more secure. He pulled out his normal phone, punching in numbers and a man answered quickly asking, "Hello, Mr. Fratto, how can I help you this evening? Do you or one of your gentleman or lady friends need my services?"

Fratto paid handsomely to have Mr. Twain on his payroll and at his beck and call. Fratto had more calls to make, especially he thought if he wanted to continue living. He said, "Get down to the Keys Jail, I want you to get Charlie Ford and two other people named Jim and Tim out. They would have been booked at the exact same time. If the guy at the front desk tries to give you any shit, please tell him I would consider it a personal favor if he could help you expedite the process of finding out their first and last names so you can retain them as your clients."

"Certainly, Mr. Fratto, is this something that should be easy for me to handle? Is this time-sensitive?"

"Mr. Twain, for what I pay you, there should be zero doubts from me ever that there's anything you wouldn't be able to handle. If that has changed over the years, please let me know. I need the best and living representation that I can get. Actually, after you get these three boys out, you take them somewhere and call me when you get there. Any of the homes would be adequate to go to".

Mr. Twain probably already knew the answer, but he hadn't gotten into positions like this by being an idiot. He said, "Am I in any danger, sir? Are you in any danger, sir?"

"Mr. Twain, the chances of us getting through the next day without needing your services at some point are slim to none. But everything should be okay."

"I just hope that you're being transparent with me, sir. There's little that I can do to protect you if I'm dead. Does that seem fair, sir?"

"Yes, Mr. Twain. I'm confident that there's enough going on tonight that you and the other three will be just fine. I feel like I'll have all of the attention for everyone so that'll leave you free to roam the city and make it somewhere safe."

Mr. Twain had a considerable number of questions still, but he had been under Mr. Fratto providing his special niche services, being retained for quite some time now, to know what the issues were most of the time. Mr. Twain said, "I'm aware that this evening is not going as you wish, sir. Is there anything else that I need to know?"

Fratto was pushing in more slugs as he drove and replied, "Yes, there's probably a lot we should talk about, Mr. Twain. However, I don't have time for it."

"I suspect we should have plenty of time to talk later, sir. Stay well and we shall talk later."

Fratto liked the way this guy talked. He didn't know too many people that had that silver tongue way about him, but Mr. Twain seemed like that's the only way he'd ever spoken. If that wasn't the way he'd been his entire life, then he was one hell of a bullshit artist. Fratto tucked his phone back in his suit breast pocket, still somewhat trying to figure shit out as the different scenarios were coming across his plate. He truly was more than a little nervous about everything and how it was all transpiring. The word smooth was not something he would use from a vocabulary sense to explain anything about tonight.

Fratto could see lights in his rear view were coming from what seemed like everywhere. He was pretty sure that this was not going to be kosher. The lights stayed consistent behind him, and he started to push the car to an above-average speed, going far over the speed limit. Fratto kept looking and kept realizing they were definitely getting closer by the second. The busy street he'd been on had gotten quieter and less full of innocent bystanders.

He tried making a few quick turns to put some distance between them. Unfortunately, all that it did was let them catch up. But it did clarify that he really was being followed and that it wasn't in his head. It wasn't some sort of paranoia with his mind playing tricks on him. Fratto, always the boss, actually laughed because the vehicles all looked the same. That was something he thought was quite idiotic, to tell the truth.

He never had an entire crew with the same car. It only made things too easy and too simple to know immediately that it was someone in his crew. The SUVs raced, trying to catch up until they were close enough to almost be able to give detailed descriptions on the driver and passenger. Fratto knew that this car could take a licking and slammed both feet down on the brakes. Something the man who had put his window down and stuck himself outside of the vehicle had not been counting on. The moment that he began braking was also the moment in which he would either be killed or shopping for a wheelchair. The man bounced out of the front seat, landing on the hot highway below, and Fratto was pretty sure he just broke his back or spine or both. One thing that was for sure was he would feel this in the morning and a few after. He knew some friends that had got motorcycle road rash and could assume this was severely worse.

The man who was directly behind Fratto driving began firing out the window. He sent an entire magazine in Fratto's direction. Whatever had been left of the glass in the rear of the car was now just pieces of fragments on the ground. Two SUVs came up, trying to box him in. The shooting behind him, at least, had stopped for the moment. He knew that was going to be short-lived, though. Fratto saw the two vehicles on either side inching up. He could only assume that they thought this was their big power play. Fratto waited until the windows were down and the muzzles of the guns could be seen before punching the gas.

The car on the left had already begun shooting and hadn't expected Fratto to accelerate as quickly as he did. He let off an entire magazine from what he could only assume was a modified handgun unless these guys truly did have machine guns which wouldn't really surprise Fratto all that much. The man hit home with every shot, but home was a bit off target. The man driving took the brunt of the gunfire. He fell forward on the wheel pushing it to the left. The driver who'd been behind Fratto did not fare well.

Fratto pulled out his crew phone, punching speed dial for Phil, a guy that had been with him longer than his only son Junior had been alive. One thing about calling someone on the crew was they did not send him to voicemail. It did not matter if you were at a baptism for your child, your wife was having a baby or a million other reasons which did not matter; if he called, you answered. If you wanted to make the big easy money, then that meant there were no sick days.

A gruff voice that probably had smoked too many cigarettes for too long answered on the second ring. He had learned long ago that even though his boss seemed like a pretty good guy, all in all, Phil had seen him do some absolutely gruesome shit that he easily could have had anyone on the crew take care of. He always had to question just a little in the back of his mind if it was because he liked it, or because he wanted to make sure that there wasn't a shortage of fear about what would happen, with examples of course, if anyone ever decided that being unfaithful would be the more appealing option.

Fratto said, "Where are you?"

The man answered, not sure at this time of night without anything on their plans what the issue was. He was always watching his back and immediately ran through the last week or two in his head, trying to remember what if anything he did would have pissed-off the boss. But there was nothing that came to mind. He replied, "I was picking up a couple pies and then headed over to Frank's, you know, for poker night. Are you going to clean us out, Mr. Fratto?"

"Forget the pizzas; I want you to come meet me at a location that I'm going to text you. When you get there, you come heavy!"

"Who else do you want me to bring with me?"

"Did I say anything about bringing anyone else with you?"

"No, you didn't, sir."

"Then why the fuck are you asking me who I want you to bring with?"

"Is everything all right, Mr. Fratto?"

"Jesus Christ, Phil, use some intuition. Think about it for a minute. Maybe answer that question for yourself. Calling late at night, I told you to come heavy, told you to come alone, I guess what other warning signs do you need?"

Phil was not ignorant. He knew being on the good side of someone versus the latter was not the worst thing to do in the world of criminal activity. He simply replied, "I just need the address, Mr. Fratto. Hell, tell me a direction to head and I'll start going that way."

"Just start heading towards the hoity-toity area of the Keys, that new shopping district."

"I can do that. You sure you don't want me to send any of the boys over to your house for the missus or to pick up Junior?"

Fratto didn't answer but hit the end on the phone. He drove for another ten minutes before finding a secluded spot where he could see with his own eyes if someone was coming. He sent Phil the message and sat back and waited.

Chapter 7

Charlie walked back to a cell. When he passed by Tim and Jim, he said the same thing to each of them, "Don't worry about a lawyer. I got it covered."

Tim kind of sat there for a moment waiting for more words to come, preferably ones that would make him feel better. When Charlie didn't say anything else, he yelled, "I don't even know what the hell that means? How do you have it covered? I thought that you were going to call…"

Charlie yelled, "Jesus Christ, just trust me, Tim!"

Tim held up his hands saying, "Okay then. Charlie's got it handled. You the man."

The jailer looked at Jim and Tim saying, "So do you two want your phone call?"

Jim said, "No, I had a pretty big dinner. I think I'll wait till morning, call Leslie's Diner up, maybe have them drop off some eggs, bacon, hash browns, toast maybe a couple pancakes, oh, and some coffee. Just do the whole works, you know? I'll have you bring it back here and the food is on me. You'll have to give me my wallet though, I don't think that they work on the barter system at our diner."

The jailer smiled but it didn't put anyone at ease as he nodded his head rolling a toothpick across his lips in between his teeth and said, "Ya know I have a feeling after tonight you probably aren't going to be able to trade much for sex. I mean if they're going off of looks. You boys have a good night."

Jim knew he should shut up, but it wasn't going to change any outcomes if he did. He said, "Jailer, just a quick question?"

The Jailer turned around and he wasn't amused. He said, "What? What the hell do you want?"

"I just wanted to confirm something, so you're saying right now you do consider me attractive right? I mean it doesn't have to be sexual. I'm just asking, you know, as a friend. Like, am I, McCartney or Lennon, in your eyes?"

The jailer just smiled, turned around, and kept walking. Jim waited until the jailer had left and yelled to Tim and Charlie, "So, I think these guys are going to be our new best friends."

Tim had already sized up the two men in his cell. Between the two of them, unfortunately, they each were almost the same size as he was. Both of them obviously spent some time hanging out in the weight room. Except, these guys looked like they probably had prison or gang tattoos versus his Naval-themed designs.

Tim had never sat down once he got in his cell. He looked at the two men, gauging before finally saying, "Well if all of you guys are going to get to it then let's fucking do it. It's been a long goddamn day, and quite frankly, I could use a nap."

One of the two men in Tim's cell obviously thought he was quite the warrior. He said, "Do you really think sleeping with the two of us in here is going to be a good idea?"

Tim smiled; he wasn't confident or cocky. He was trained, and quite frankly, that was a big difference from some people out there. You could have all the muscle in the world, but it didn't do a goddamn thing if you didn't know when and how to use it. Tim replied, "It's probably not a wise idea to sleep with two guys like you sharing my cell. But I like to think once you two are sleeping it won't be an issue."

The man smiled; even in the shitty lighting of the jail cell, there was a small reflection coming off of his gold tooth that Tim had to question if it was real or not. He replied, "Well, you guys will be sleeping. So, it's not going to be a large concern of mine."

The two men stood, puffing up their chests and arms as if it would do something to somehow help them. They definitely were going to try and intimidate him. Tim realized that no one had told the guy behind him that blonde ponytails, even as greasy as his were, were not scary in the least. The talker of the two, Mr. Gold tooth said, "Well, we aren't tired, and we aren't taking a nap anytime soon."

Tim smiled with no gold teeth, because he wasn't a loser, and said, "Well, I guess I might have used the wrong phrase there, friend. I meant to say you'll be going to sleep once I put you down for the count. Does that sound a little bit more accurate to you? I could probably take all six of you out. But that's probably not going to be possible."

Gold tooth man cut Tim off, apparently thinking his words were still going to do something, and said, "Damn right you're not going to take all six of us out. Because the two of us are gonna kick your black ass."

Tim nodded, shaking off his state-issued flip-flops to get ready for what would come next, and said, "Oh yeah, it's as black as the night. But the reason I'm not going to kick the shit out of the other four is you know because unlike you I'm not a fucking idiot. See, I am well aware that I'm in a jail cell and can't reach the other two or the other two on the far end. But I am pretty confident here that my friends will take care of that for me. When the jailer comes back, you make sure you ask for a bonus, because you're gonna fucking need it. There's no way you are putting yourself at this much of a risk without compensation."

Gold tooth raced up to Tim, looking like he was going to throw a UFC haymaker at him. Tim didn't so much as flinch, he waited for the punch which could not have been telegraphed more. When the man's fist was within about two inches of his face, Tim sidestepped him, realizing the ponytail guy was not waiting his turn like a gentleman. Tim couldn't blame him, even his friend knew his punch wasn't going to connect. But his own punch selection seemed to think that throwing a straight punch was going to be the way to take out this giant of a man. Tim was as limber as he was strong and brought a front snap kick directly up into the man's chin. The clicking noise of his teeth smashing together was cringe-worthy.

The ponytail guy stumbled backward, smashing his head back against the brick wall. Much like the wall not giving any cushion, it also did not provide the other four men with a plethora of hope that they would be successful in this endeavor. Mr. Gold tooth, who Tim had sidestepped, crashed face first, or actually fist first, into the jail cell bars. The crack of knuckle on steel was not ideal. It wasn't going to take a doctor to know that he'd just messed up his hand severely.

The man screamed as loud as he could when his fist slammed into the bars. He'd felt plenty of pain in his life, but this, he was pretty confident, was his first time ever breaking his hand. The worst part about it was it was his own fault and he'd used his own strength to break it. Tim walked the few steps quickly to where the gold tooth guy was somewhat stuck in the jail cell bars. Tim put his leg back behind the man's legs and used his right hand to grip him by the throat and forced him back as hard as he could, giving him no chance to do anything but to land on his ass and to do so hard.

Ponytail guy was starting to get up off the ground. Tim knelt down, untying, and pulling the boot off his foot. They were steel-toed leather work boots that Tim didn't think had probably ever seen any actual employment while wearing. He waited for the man to come at him and brought up the large boot, holding it by the part that went around the upper ankle and back towards him as hard as he could, striking him directly in the face with the steel toe.

Tim, never one to take the half-ass route, continued striking him in the face with it until blood and teeth began dribbling from his mouth. The man held up his hands in a plea that he could take no more. Tim, not knowing how long he was going to be in here with these two, didn't think compassion was a good sign to show. He dropped the boot. The man's hands were quivering out in front of him. Dropping the boot had actually looked like he had a little bit of hope because of it.

Tim squashed that hope with a haymaker of his own directly into the man's already bruising and swelling cheek. He didn't go down for the count after the first punch, but Tim came back with a left hook snapping his head over drool and teeth still continuing to come out, spraying the dingy white walls of the jail cell. When he didn't think he could take any more pain, the final blow of an uppercut with all Tim's might came, striking him beneath the chin, and effectively without question turned out his lights.

The shoeless man on the ground with the broken hand truly did not know what to do. They'd been sent here for what obviously had not been nearly enough money. Not nearly enough at all. He was trying to think what weapon he had on him that would be useful but was unsure of his answer. He tried to get up as Tim brought back a foot, kicking him three times in the ribs as hard as he could with all his might. The man grunted and screamed with each kick until Tim was pretty sure he had just fractured at least two or three of his ribs. He had had to deal with that previously and knew this guy wasn't going to get up and do anything quickly for months.

The man curled up in the fetal position. Tim took a hold of his hair, lifting his head up and bringing a final one, and punched back down into his skull. Tim walked over to the sink, washing the blood from his knuckles, thinking that these guys definitely didn't know what they had gotten themselves into.

Jim whistled saying, "Did you guys see that? Holy shit, he just kicked the shit out of your friends. Did you see that seriously? Those guys were big and had muscles and tattoos and really looked scary, what with their blonde ponytails and gold tooth. He just made them his bitches. Not even his first one, like his third bitch down, you know, the earner. I'm gonna start calling him Pimpin' Tim. What do you guys think about that? Jesus, he's the pussy of the group, too. You guys didn't even take him out, what the hell's wrong with you? Is that why you are here? To get beaten up?"

Apparently, the men still thought they had a chance. Jim could only assume they, much like the two in Charlie's jail cell, were going to do nothing but underestimate. Jim asked, "So tell me, did you guys want to come after me first? Otherwise, were you going to go after my pal Charlie there first, fellows? Otherwise, you can start with me, just be gentle, I'm a fragile Irish ginger."

Charlie felt like he was in the principal's office, waiting to have detention handed out to him. Much like a shot or pulling off a band-aid, he'd rather just get it done over having to wait. He figured if these guys were stupid enough to come after him, then they were stupid enough to pay for it and take any means required that he had to do to protect himself, maybe just short of killing them.

The last thing he wanted to do was have a legit reason to stay in the Florida Keys jail system. The two groups of men who were still able to stand of their own free will didn't get a choice in who was going to fight first. Charlie ran up to the first one, catching them off guard. It would seem they thought that their advantage would be enough to help them. However, that was absolutely not the case. Charlie, never one to mince words, came straight up, punching the first one directly in the nose. Charlie was thinking that he was getting pretty fucking good at breaking people's noses. He wasn't sure where he was on his count, but he was thinking he was five for five right now. Although he would like to try and forget about the ass whooping he'd taken, but in his defense, it had been a beat down, not necessarily mano a mano fight.

The man didn't even have time to duck; when Charlie connected, he held nothing about it back. The man instantly covered his nose, trying to protect it from the pain as if his fingers would do something magical to make it feel better. Charlie throat-punched the guy, bringing him down to his knees gasping for air. He realized pretty quickly that he'd forgotten or hyper-focused on the guy in front of him. Charlie was pivoting to do a roundhouse kick into the side of his head when a worn leather belt came in front of his eyes and instantly became tight as could be around his neck. Charlie's plans changed instantly.

Charlie tried getting a hand up before Mr. Belt guy was able to tighten it against his neck. He was too late though, and to make matters even shittier, the man stuck the end of the belt through the buckle until he made it feel like a noose tightening more by the second around Charlie's neck. Charlie was never out looking to cause pain. But right now, if he could kill Mr. Belt guy, he'd be just fine with it. Jim and Tim stared, feeling helpless and not loving the fact that they were separated; even though it was only six feet away, it might as well have been a hundred miles, for all the good that they could do for him right now. The man with the belt yelled to his cellmate, "Get your ass up now! Help me finish this fucker. We get extra if we make sure he doesn't walk out of this jail cell."

Charlie was sure feeling honored at this point that he was getting so much special attention, even though ninety-nine percent of it was purely because they wanted to kill him. The man was still coughing on the ground, grabbing his throat and his nose with the other hand, trying to find a way to make either of them feel better. When he finally stumbled up from the ground, Charlie backed up, pushing the man who had the belt noose around his neck up against the bars. Charlie was starting to see spots in his vision. He reached behind him, putting his hands around the man's neck, and using all of his muscle to hold himself up.

The man tried shaking his grip off, moving them forward a few feet, but Charlie was gripping onto every ounce of skin that he could and not letting up for anything. He brought up both feet, glad that he had kicked the flip flops off, which were pointless other than to avoid getting athlete's foot in the shower. He snapped his legs forward, sending both heels into throat punch guy's face. He tried to move, but his reflexes weren't what they needed to be. Just being able to stand wasn't going to cut it.

The double kick propelled Charlie and leather belt guy backward, crashing leather belt guy's head into the cell bars. Charlie, as soon as he had put his legs down, let go of the man's neck, using what small number of nails that he had to drag them across either side of his neck and didn't stop scraping until his fingers touched. Charlie didn't know if he'd leave a scar, but he definitely would remember him for quite a few days. The scrape had an added bonus: it made the leather belt guy turn into 'nothing in his hands' guy.

The man lost his grip on the belt. Charlie fell forward and put his feet down before the man began sliding down to the ground on the bars. He pulled it off of his neck, sucking in a deep breath, still feeling the tautness of the belt pulsating where it'd been tight. The receiver of the kick had bounced off the wall and slid down onto the toilet. The upside of this was the fact that he'd let go of the belt, giving Charlie just long enough to get the belt removed from his neck, giving him a chance to take in a deep breath and try to figure things out just as quickly as he possibly could what to do next.

Nothing in his hands guy cringed as he touched his neck, seeing blood on both of his hands knowing exactly what it was from. He yelled, "You're fucking dead! When I get my hands on you, I'm going to tear you a new asshole."

Jim, from the other cell, said, "Is it the new asshole that's gonna kill him?"

The man snapped, not really thinking about it before yelling, "You're next, motherfucker. You better shut the fuck up!"

Jim shrugged and pointed, saying "But there's bars. You actually can't kill me, cuz there's bars. These douchebags could try, but I'm hoping after Charlie finishes beating the shit out of your friends that they just decide to maybe let bygones be bygones. What do you think?"

The two men in the cell were seriously considering their odds given what was going on with their friends. But they murmured to each other, trying to figure out if they should do anything. If that answer was yes, then what was it that they should do? They decided to wait it out until they knew what was going on with Charlie's cell.

When the man with the bloody neck scarf started to get up, Charlie took the slotted end of the belt tightly around his hand and whipped the belt directly into the man's face, tearing at his cheeks when the metal hooks of the belt buckle found his flesh. Charlie didn't so much as cringe when he hit him. He quite frankly couldn't have been fucking happier about it. The man tried squinting, but in a matter of about five seconds, Charlie had hit him three additional times in the face as hard as he could with a leather belt. The promise of welts were already forming on both of his cheeks.

When the man who'd been catching a breather laying on the toilet tried getting up, Charlie walked forward, kicking him in the face, and this time he truly did collapse on the toilet. Charlie rested a foot on the man's head, pushing him down beneath the water line. He wrapped the leather strap around the pipe at the bottom of the toilet, submerging the man's face in the water and tying it off. Charlie flushed the toilet once showing the man that dying wasn't actually necessary but that he sure as hell wasn't going to be going anywhere anytime soon.

The original one with the new claw marks and belt whips across his face for some reason and decided to try and come at Charlie one last time. He waited for the man to throw a punch and stepped to the side, throwing the hardest punch that he could after taking the man's arm and buried one hell of a hook into his elbow. The sound of the bone-breaking echoed through the cells and the man screamed like a five-year-old girl.

Charlie spun the man around, slamming him face-first into the jail bars, and didn't stop until the only thing holding him up was Charlie. Charlie shook his hands out, glad that he did not break them on the off chance that they had additional douche bags to put in the jail cells with them. Jim smiled saying, "It's your last chance, fellows. I know I'm pretty, but I am one mean Irish motherfucker. Let bygones be bygones, eh? We could spoon. I'm not going to be in the middle though, I have standards. I don't like getting poked with objects, even though I would assume yours are probably kind of tiny."

The two men in their defense did take a moment to consider if this was maybe something that they did not actually need to commit to. They were thinking no one could actually blame them if they backed off and didn't go through, given what had just transpired. Jim was smiling, but on the inside, he was already thinking about thirty different ways he could take these two out without so much as breaking a sweat.

Tim was watching and waiting, trying to think of anything he might mention to Jim to let him know if there was an option for him to help take them out. Nothing was coming to mind. One of the men reached down to his belt, taking it off and wrapping the leather around his knuckles. The other pushed some buttons on his belt buckle and pulled out what looked like a little dagger that was supposed to be quite intimidating, they figured. Jim said, "No shit? Seriously, is that real? Oh my god, I can't believe that you actually have that. Was it free? I mean did someone ask you to buy it on a crazy challenge? I mean it, I got to know is it sharp?"

The man who thought he could be cocky said, "You can tell me when I shove it through your jugular."

Jim said, "Is that in my neck?"

"I mean, I'm just gonna try and figure out where you want to get all stabby on me."

The man with the belt said, "Do you ever shut up?"

Without hesitation, Tim said, "Not in the ten plus years that I've known him. Not one fucking time; not even asleep. The son of a bitch snores."

Jim said, "You don't need to share our drama with the likes of these fellows. Now I guess we should probably get on with this otherwise there's still the option of spooning. I am a little sleepy. I won't lie."

The two men rushed him, thinking that having two of them with the weapons would be enough to help take him out. Unfortunately for the two that were trying to deal with Jim, now they had their hopes at an all-time low. Watching four of their constituents absolutely get pummeled by the other two men had not been an uplifting experience for anyone's spirits. Charlie figured anyone who didn't have to deal with Tim probably thought that they were special, but unfortunately as well for them, no one knew Jim had been a middleweight boxing champ in the Navy. Tim had seen him beat the shit out of more people in a fight than he could probably count on one hand. It was definitely a good reason to always have Jim on your side. He could easily hold his own and at the same time make it look pretty fucking easy.

Jim had already gone into a boxing stance, hands up, and since he was a righty he had his left foot forward, and much like Tim and Charlie, had already kicked off the pointless and useless flip flops. The two men hesitated a little as typically only an insane person would be smiling at his two would-be attackers who took off racing the very short distance straight for Jim. He made a little kissing sound for them, only pouring fuel on that fire. Tim and Charlie of course were not surprised given the fact that as they had seen him kick the hell out of so many people; they had also seen him piss off more people than one person could count.

Jim's reflexes were not slow in any way at all. That moment that they made it up to him, Jim knew he only cared about the knife dagger thing. He didn't personally order his self-defense items from Amazon, but alas he wasn't going to complain if those coming for him did. Knife guy tried lunging forward with his knife. Unfortunately for the two of them, they could only grip around what wasn't faster than their own reflexes.

Jim had kept a few feet between himself and the jail cell. It wasn't very easy to throw a legit punch when you had a wall behind you. For some reason each of the men were thinking the one on the left would get the left hand to punch and the one on the right...you do the math. Jim brought a straight punch with his right hand into the left man's jaw, connecting Irish knuckles to the loser's face perfectly. The man didn't go down, but his stabby motion went to shit.

He tripped forward, sending his hand through the bars still with the cheap dagger in his hand. Leather belt hand guy was looking at him, trying to gauge what was next. That decision was made when Jim had a left hook going straight across and just waiting for the guy to get there. This one did send him to the ground, or at least halfway because his torso landed on one of the two beds in the jail cell. Jim was just getting loose and asked, "Wait, so are you saying you do want to spoon? You just aren't all the way up on the bed, so I just can't tell. Are you playing hard to get? Is that why you are on your knees? I'm sorry; it isn't my thing."

Charlie and Tim both knew how damn annoying Jim could be when he wanted to, as well sometimes when he wasn't trying. But they each couldn't help but smile, knowing that these guys had to be absolutely infuriated given the fact that not only did they have to listen to Jim's shit, they also were getting their asses kicked by him. No man enjoyed having his manhood questioned and this guy wasn't any different. Before he could get up, dagger guy said, "I'm going to fucking kill you. I promise…"

Jim smiled and debated rushing the guy before he could bring his arm out, lifting his leg and unapologetically snapping it down and breaking the man's arm. But Jim didn't think he needed to go quite that far. They were yet to land a punch or kick, so he wasn't super concerned. He took a step back, motioning for the belt buckle knife guy to get up. By now, the other guy had tried to push up off of the cot-like bed, but before he had a chance to fully get up, Jim had already brought down a wicked right hand into the top of his eyebrow. Something this guy apparently didn't know but Jim obviously did, was especially when fighting barehanded, a good shot to the temple was almost always a great way to make someone bleed. This guy was absolutely not any different. He hit him so hard that he fell over to the side, and Jim asked, "Hey, you've got a little blood there, man. Have you been with any dirty women by chance? Is there anything I need to worry about? Would I need to get tested?"

The man wanted to get up but currently, he was seeing three or four of everything he was looking at. What he did see had a shade of red to it from his seemingly never-ending wound. He lay there for a moment looking at his partner saying, "Are you going to get up?"

The man was really trying to decide if this was worth it. Belt buckle guy snapped, yelling, "This is all your fucking fault, you know. I didn't want to do this job, and you just fucking suck. We sure as shit aren't getting paid nearly enough for any of this; I mean it. Would you look at your face and mine, what the hell am I going to do about this?"

The man was trying to hold his head, but blood was gushing from the wound and from in between his fingers. He asked, "Do you want to just quit now? Maybe just leave? Good luck with that, you're locked in a fucking jail cell, you idiot. Get your ass up and do something now! You've got two arms."

The man had very little interest in going back down to the floor again. He knew each time that he did it was probably going to get much worse. Of course, he wasn't sure what worse was going to be but at the same time didn't want to find out. He did know that he really hated this son of a bitch. Jim smiled, motioning for the guy to get up…if he dared, but he was more than ready for him when he did rise.

Belt buckle guy reached in between the bars and got the knife and hoped with it he would find his confidence builder back. He rushed Jim, staying low, trying to avoid his fists. He was very confident by now that the stranger that looked like he'd been a boxer probably had been. That moment that he thought he actually had a good chance at this diminished very quickly. Jim smiled, motioning for him to come at him, and the guy raced towards Jim, expecting a punch of some sort. Belt buckle dude lunged forward with the knife. Most normal people would be scared, would move, hell they might even flinch. Jim just kept on smiling, and when he lunged forward trying to stab him in the gut, Jim took his wrist, spinning him around in a circle, and no one understood what they did, but his feet and head traded places as Jim flipped him into the air. He landed on his back on the cold hard cement floor. Jim bent down, picked up the knife, and stuck it in his back pocket. He didn't need it for a fool like this.

The apparent boss of the group looked down and could not have been less impressed with the makeshift crew he'd assembled. He knew those in charge of everything were going to absolutely not be impressed. Not impressed in the slightest; if he lived through this then he would be equally impressed if he lived through the next day once they were released. Jim got in the middle of the cell saying, "Are we done, or what's going on?"

Tim yelled, "Hey, just an idea. I know you're not an intelligent ex-Naval police officer like us, but maybe see who they're working for."

Jim got the guy over bringing up a fist yelling, "Yeah that's a really good idea. Who are you working for, douchebag?"

The man replied, "Go fuck yourself."

"Is that Bosnian or Russian? I couldn't even handle Spanish, but my God I love Spanish women. It's something about their passion. You know what I'm talking about in the sheets. However, I don't know who that is I mean how do you get a hold of go fuck yourself?"

"You're gonna die. You're gonna die when you get out of here, goddamn it. There's money on your fucking heads, You just wait."

Jim replied, "Well of course they're gonna have to wait. I mean there's six of you and three of us and you guys couldn't even hit one of us, let alone kill us. Do you have one of those really neat knives as well, or was the belt your big-ticket item?"

"I'm not going to say anything about who I work for."

Jim pulled the knife out of his back pocket. He asked, "Wait...wait...wait, are you sure, I mean would it be easier if maybe I was to put this knife through your leg, or gut, or...I don't know there's probably a lot of places I could put it. Is your employer going to do anything here to save you? I mean was continuing to bleed your main goal because kudos, you are doing the best."

"You won't last a day when you get out."

"Geez, here I thought you'd take me out way quicker than that. You're going to get some medical care before you decide to come after me, is that why I'll last so long, or do you just enjoy repeating yourself?"

He took a telegraphed swing towards Jim who took a step back. He was starting to feel offended about the attempt these guys were putting into this. Jim popped him quickly with a jab to the nose. He shouldn't have mocked Jim; he knew how hard to punch if he wanted to damage someone. The guy was stupid enough to say, "Is that all you got? Christ how'd you take two of us down with pussy ass punches..."

Jim took hold of his shirt, smiling, and swung a quick upper cut into his ribs, and before he could bend over to hold himself in a way that didn't hurt, a pretty pissed-off Jim took the boss by his ears, and with lightning speed, brought up a knee directly into his nose. He stumbled backward, trying to catch his balance. The cell boss didn't know if he should hold his nose or ribs. When Jim took a step toward him, his tough-guy act melted. He held up his hands, trying not to cry, but the toughest guy getting hit in the nose was in no way abnormal. Jim asked, "Oh, were you ready to…"

Tim yelled, "Jim, Christ, let him talk. Shut up."

"Fine, I'll shut up. Who are you working for?"

"Look, the detective has us on stand-by if he needs something done, then he asks us to check in for a few days. We get some pay, we get out, and at some point, he calls us back up, gives us some perks in the community."

"You feeling real good about everything right now, I mean are these the perks you were hoping for?"

"It'll be our last time having two guys. I can assure you that you've made someone else's life a helluva lot shittier by what I've learned today."

"I don't think that you learned shit tonight if you are still planning on this being part of your yearly income. You don't seem to understand how bad you are at this job. If you were good at it, maybe you'd be okay, but look at the six of you, I think you're the only one awake so far. That's only because I didn't knock you the fuck out. Was it Lindvall, is that the detective?"

"He's the only one in the Keys that matters. Now leave me alone so I can bleed in silence."
Jim looked back yelling, "Hey, good news guys, it's a crooked cop. Same one it seems that arrested us. Do you think that's a good

thing or not so much?"

Tim just rubbed his hands on his face. He didn't like dirty cops, especially dirty cops currently in charge of his future. He was seriously starting to wonder if pulling the anchor up on Charlie's boat and the three of them sailing off to a more peaceful place would be an intelligent idea. It definitely would alleviate some of the shit going on if they were to go. He knew they could go forever in that boat, and the chances were better than fair that it would run like a champ. Charlie said, "He's not going to do anything stupid, or anything else stupid. He knows we've got that evidence and that isn't something that he's going to want any outside agencies seeing."

"Guy like that isn't going to let you hang a threat over him forever," Jim replied.

"So, as of now, we are potentially going to have to worry about Bruno and Lou, not a huge deal and that's if they don't go to the hospital first. I am pretty sure if Lou has his way that it will definitely be a stop once they get back to shore. I hope the fucks had to swim the entire way," Charlie said.

Tim asked, "You guys sure there's nothing to worry about big enough to not just leave town? I mean, are you going to be able to do justice for your uncle by being dead?"

"No, probably not, but at the same time I can't say for sure that I'll be able to live with myself if I run away with my tail stuck between my legs either."

Tim nodded - they were in it to win it. But the choice was Charlie's. Tim said, "Just one thing to remember, if the kids going after his own dad...you might not think it's important, but his dad might be more interested in being the one who takes care of his own son, as fucked up as that sounds."

Charlie nodded, explaining, "I don't want the son. It looks like Bruno and his crew are the ones that we really need to have a serious talk with. If I had known it was them definitively, I would have been able to probably get a few more things done when I was on that boat. I still can't believe they were stupid enough to try and turn a guy that can't be turned because he's as loyal as you could possibly ever want."

Jim said, "Well, unfortunately, thugs are absolute idiots, and these guys are like king stupid shit."

Charlie said, "Well I have a feeling that we will be doing the world a favor. Actually, I can be the one doing the good deeds. You guys don't need to be in this that deep. I could definitely handle those two on my own."

Tim asked, "Sorry if this sounds ignorant, but how exactly are you able to handle it on your own? I mean, you do remember that we came out to the middle of the ocean at night to save you because you had had your feet well soaked in cement."
Charlie snapped his fingers saying, "You know I forgot about being

kidnapped and taken out in the middle of nowhere to die. Thanks for the reminder."

Tim's smirk, knowing he was correct, made Charlie laugh all the same. Jim said, "Well, what do we want to do about the detective once we get out of there?"

Charlie said, "I don't have a good answer for that yet. Unfortunately, a dirty cop is still a cop. The last thing we need to do is to seek revenge on him and then have to deal with the repercussions after that."

Jim and Tim both gave a thumbs up and sat down looking at their handiwork bleeding on the cell floor.

Chapter 8

The door to the police station opened slowly and gently. Mr. Twain walked in carrying a leather briefcase that his wife had bought him decades ago when he had first opened up his own private practice for criminal defense. The man at the front office noticed him coming up and motioned for him as if he hadn't been there a million times before to come over to their desk.

Mr. Twain walked up, nodding. His usual pleasant demeanor was not to be seen. He was here working by the hour for, at least in his line of work, one of the best people you probably could work for. He said, "I'm here to represent three of the inmates currently being held against their will, in your jail."

The desk cop wasn't scared of lawyers and didn't feel the least bit threatened by this one...at least, not yet. The police officer said, "What are the names of the three men or women that you are here for?"

"How many do you have here today?"

"Sir, that is confidential information. I do apologize. I would like to tell you but it's not something that we are allowed to disclose for security purposes."

"Security for whom? You already have them detained and in a jail cell, don't you?"

"Sir, It's probably above your head. It's nothing personal. A lot of people have issues understanding the law."

Mr. Twain pulled out a card and handed it to the man. The officer looked at it saying, "What do I need this for?"

A man that didn't look like he could punch his way out of a paper towel took on a different look, something dark and knowledgeable in his eyes. Twain replied confidently, "Well when I finish getting these three out of jail right now and tonight, the next thing that I'm going to do is make a call to the district attorney and the governor, where I will lodge a complaint against you for failure to cooperate. You are trying to keep my clients from me, and their God-given right to counsel. You are also wasting my time, and quite frankly it's late and you're putting me in one pisser of a mood."

"Sir, it isn't that..."

"You can call me Mr. Twain, and the reason I gave you that card is so you do not forget my name. See, I'll be the one suing you for everything you've ever thought you owned or ever will own and make sure that when I'm done you're unemployed and unemployable. Does that sound preferable to you? Otherwise, do you think maybe there's a solution in the middle that we could come to? Your choice. I have nothing but time, money, and resources."

The officer quite literally could feel his balls rising up into his throat. It was not a pleasant thing whatsoever. The desk sergeant usually was not one to get intimidated. Like a good majority of police officers, they thought they would be taking absolutely zero amounts of shit from anyone, but not this guy, he knew. The man said, "Look, I really don't think I've done anything to get sued; you've only been here a few minutes."

Mr. Twain said, "The other two are Tim and Jim. So, if you can find two other inmates with that name, booked in close to at the same time or directly after Mr. Charlie Ford then I'm confident those are the two who should be coming with me as well."

"We haven't set any bail, sir?"

"Splendid, that's fantastic. What were my clients charged with that they would require bail?"

"You'd have to speak to the detective, sir. That's his department."

Twain could smell a line of bullshit a mile long. He didn't have to puff up his chest. But he did have a solid thirty-plus years of practicing, as well as reading about the law. He knew that he would forget more in his days left on Earth than this dipshit behind the desk would ever be able to fathom learning. Mr. Twain said, "You do realize you are unable to arrest someone without due cause, correct?"

The desk sergeant pulled out Charlie's file, trying to see what, if any, quick notes Lindvall had put in there. He pointed at it saying,

"Look right there. He had a disassembled firearm."

"So, would you arrest someone for having a pack of matches beneath water?"

"What does that have to do with guns?"

"It's only a functioning gun if it is put together. If it is not put together, then it is just a bunch of parts. Now, my clients did not have firearms put together. As well how do you even know that the gun works if it was not assembled? It might have been a project piece. But it does not matter in this case. Now, did they strike the officer?"

"No, and it was a detective, but there was no violence."

"Were there complaints lodged against my clients?"

The desk sergeant could see where this was going. When in doubt, he knew it was better to ask for forgiveness than to make stupid choices. He said, "Just give me one second, please. I need to make a call."

He didn't let a pissed-off Twain keep him from hitting the speed dial for his chief. The chief answered on the third ring. The chief had definitely been sleeping and wasn't super excited when he answered the phone. He said, "Is someone dead?"

"No, it's worse…"

The chief already had a feeling he knew what was going on. He asked, "Is it a lawyer?"

"Yeah, there was an arrest tonight..."

"A police officer or detective made an arrest...oh do tell."

"It was Lindvall, sir..."

"Of course, it was Lindvall. When isn't it? Do I need to come down there, Scott? Does he actually have anything on them"

"I'd say it is pretty loose. There are disassembled weapons, a possible violence charge, possible breaking, and entering, but the witness aka victim did not want to report anything at..."

"Jesus Christ, he usually does a little better job than that of trying to make sure shits gonna stick. What in the fuck was he thinking, damn it?"

"What did you want me to do?"

"Well, what I would like to do is take my size 11 shoe and stick it up his ass. Then I'm going to pull it back out and stick it up your ass. You do realize I was sleeping, god damn it. Do you know how long it takes for those pills to kick in so I can get a goddamn decent night's rest? No, you don't because you have a fucking peaceful easy job sitting at a goddamn desk."

"Sir, I don't…"

"That was not a rhetorical question. Do me a favor, let him see the three men."

"He doesn't want to see the three men."

"Then what the fuck does he want?"

"He wants to leave here with them."

"So, there's no reason why he arrested them, even less reason why they should be in there, and to make matters worse, there's nothing you can say that is intelligent why they ought to stay? Did you really have to call me to figure all this out?"

"There's just one last thing, sir."

"Are you trying to make sure I don't go back to sleep tonight, Scott?"

"No, sir, I swear this is the last thing. You see Lindvall called some people to take care of these guys in the holding area. Well, they've been back there for a while now, I figured I'd just leave them be and let things work out but if the three of them that he's supposed to talk to or get out are on the floor dead or knocked out then what would you like me to do?"

"I think you can probably just do me a huge favor."

"Anything, sir."

"Just shoot yourself but first go back and shoot the three of them with your gun. It will leave me with a minimal amount of paperwork to worry about."

He was going to say something when the sound of a click was all the desk sergeant could hear. Any other time, he would have happily given the phone the finger, but Twain, Mr. Twain, he thought, did not look pleased at all. The desk cop, Scott said, "If you could just bear with me one moment, Mr. Twain. I'll go back and bring the three men into an interrogation room so you can have a conversation with them."

"You can go get my three men, and then you can promptly sign them out of this jail as free men. You can also stop wasting my god damn time. If Detective Lindvall has any issues about that whatsoever all that they need to do is call that number on the card that I gave you. The one when I mentioned how I would make your life an absolute living hell and we can communicate by the phone."

"Sir, I don't know if Lindvall would be happy about talking on the phone."

"That's fine, if he'd rather talk to me in a goddamn courtroom then that would be absolutely fine. Is that what you are thinking is the way to go here?"

The desk sergeant called the jailer again and thought about curling up into a ball, hiding, and then if he was lucky, dying beneath his desk. He gave a big thumbs up to Mr. Twain, who was waiting impatiently. Now he was a little bit more worried about what might have happened to the three men who he could only assume had powerful, well-to-do friends in the Keys. He waited, unsure what this lawyer would do if something had happened to them. Scott really didn't want to imagine because it didn't seem great.

The jailer walked back to get the three men. When he opened the door, he absolutely didn't see what he had expected. The three men that he expected to be found lifeless on the floor bloodied and near death, seemed to be for the most part in perfect health. The worst-looking one was definitely Ford, but he was pretty sure that that's what he'd looked like when he'd gotten there. He walked down the cells, slowly cringing as he went by Tim's cell first, followed by Jim's, and finally Charlie's. The other men were still out for the count. Charlie and his constituents were resting, sitting on a bed in their cells, leaning back against the wall with their crossed feet stretched out on the bed. The jailer, who obviously had not had this happen previously, started yelling, "What the fuck happened here? What the fuck did you do?"

Jim couldn't resist saying, "I said the exact same thing, officer. I mean it, I said what did we do, why are we here? And you would never believe that that Lindvall guy read us our rights and brought us to jail. We couldn't be less guilty and probably deserve sainthood at some point."

"You shut the fuck up, redhead. Goddamnit, I'm serious."

Jim popped up to his feet, snapping his reacquired flip flop down on the floor and crossing his arms. Jim said, "Goddamnit, I'm serious too. We were just sitting here talking about breakfast and then BAM, this guy's head split open. This guy broke his nose. I've never seen such crazy shit in all my life. Can you believe that? These guys should have been locked up."

"No, I absolutely can't believe it."

Charlie cleared his throat saying, "Officer, if you wanted to just review the tape for the security cameras back here, I'm sure that that would be an option."

The officer knew if they did have cameras that there would be a lot of shit that would not go well for them. In this case, having additional men who weren't supposed to be in here, who also weren't arrested for anything, and had done so more than once would not be ideal in front of the right judge, he thought. The jailer sat there for a moment before finally asking, "Goddamnit, do they need medical attention?"

Jim, who was having a great time screwing with him said, "Well, I like to think when your head explodes out of nowhere that you should probably get a doctor. Maybe at the very least, a shitty nurse. You know a priest might be smart...just in case there are demons."

The officer gently put his hand on a baton pulling it out, really guessing and thinking that is what he should do to Jim. It would seem he thought beating the holy fuck out of him would probably make him feel better. Jim smiled asking, "Is that big, long black stick for me, sir?"

The jailer turned around going back to Tim's cell first. Thinking it'd be just as easy as anything working his way down. In his eyes, they were still prisoners of the Florida Keys Prison System until they were out of here, so he knew cuffs would be ideal. Tim knew the routine...he was just used to and happier with being on the other side of it. Once Tim was taken care of, he moved down to Jim. Jim whispered over his shoulder lovingly, "Be gentle, please, I'm a fragile man."

The jailer apparently hadn't encountered too many Jims in his life. That was something currently he was thinking that did not make him sad. He did make sure to put his on just a hair shy of cutting off circulation. Charlie did not put his hands through the cell and for whatever reason was the only guy smart enough to ask, "What are you doing with us? You've already got us in jail."

"I don't have to tell you a goddamn thing. Now you can either stay here, or you can stick your skinny ass arms through the cell and let me handcuff you."

"Could you give me a hint?"

"Sure, someone wants to talk to you three. The desk sarge said he seems pretty important; I don't know that you want to keep him waiting. I guess I don't know if it'll make a difference or not in the end."

In Charlie's mind, he was thinking that there was going to be a giant Bruno or Lou sitting out in the parking lot waiting and they'd be released and executed where they stood. This, of course, was not necessarily Charlie's finest moment, but he figured so long as he didn't actually hurt anyone, they would not be able to get him with a hell of a lot. He walked backward, sticking his hands through the jail bars. There was a rectangle of steel where prisoners got handcuffs put on and off. Charlie waited for the first cuff to attach to his wrist before spinning around, grabbing the man's arm, and twisting him so that he either had to twist or get his rotator cuff snapped in his shoulder.

The jailer screamed and Charlie reached over, getting the keys off of his belt while holding him still and unlocking his cell door. Charlie pulled the man's radio from his waistband, tucking it in his back pocket and as the jailer, with his free hand, tried using the baton, Charlie quickly blocked that, not wanting to get a broken arm. He took it, throwing the baton down the hall not necessarily thinking afterwards it was a genius idea as it clattered the entire fucking way. Charlie pushed the jailer into the cell saying, "I think you probably know these guys. Probably, a lot better than we do or ever want to. How many people are working the night shift?"

A very pissed-off and nervous jailer said, "Go fuck yourself, that's how many. You're gonna walk right out and get your dumb ass shot. I hope it was worth it whatever you guys think you're getting away with wherever you think you're fleeing to, no one can outrun a radio."

"We'll take our chances. We appreciate your support and consideration for our wellbeing, though."

Charlie briskly walked down, unlocking Jim and Tim's cell doors, and stripping their handcuffs off slamming the doors shut before anyone could begin getting up and ready to try and follow their route. Charlie didn't think a jailbreak of the men who actually were criminals was probably the most intelligent idea. He also didn't want to have to worry about round two, which he wasn't super worried about given the fact that the three of them had kicked the shit out of the six of them. If it was three on one against the bad guys, there was probably a good chance that they would die.

Tim was rubbing his wrists and shaking his head saying, "Well, this has definitely gone to the shitter very quickly. Is there a reason that we're just going to break out of jail? I don't know if you know this...you know, since you were a cop and all, but most criminals who break out are a hundred percent able to be set up to get shot."

Jim said, "Well, it's got to be safer on the outside than in here, right?"

Tim shrugged, replying, "They've got guns on the outside. At least all these fools had was belts, boots, and a shitty knife."

Charlie asked, "Do you really want to stay in here in a six-by-six cell and wait to see what they end up deciding to do with us? I mean it's not like we have anywhere that we can run. We're fucked if that's the case. Besides, what if they start adding people until they run out of room?"

Tim really hated how this night was progressing. The bikinis and beers laying out on a boat deck that they'd imagined had not just yet become reality. Tim replied, "Well, it's a horrible fucking idea, but at least if things go to absolute shit, I don't have to suck it up and say it was my horrible ass shitty idea."

Charlie said, "When we get to the doors that head out to the processing and into the lobby, run."

Jim, who was usually more on board for horrible ideas than Tim was, said, "I'm sorry, is that the whole plan? Because you only said one word, run. I mean that's it, just we're gonna run? I mean at some point we get to doors, right? We go through the doors, we get outside. You know if we don't get shot, Tim, feel free to run back. Then, once we're outside, we don't have a car or an escape route, and the precincts are kind of not in a super awesome part of town. What is the next step?"

Tim said, "Well, after Charlie and I head out first, preferably Charlie going ahead of me, then once we make it outside, we don't stop running until we find some way to get a ride somewhere."

Charlie said, "Well, this actually seems like it's turning out to be not so awesome of an idea. How do you think that the jailer would feel if we said we changed our minds, and just let him go?"

Tim said, "I would say that I still don't care for the idea of being killed by some hitman waiting out front for us. But I'm also not interested in going back to let the jailer out and then be beaten half to death by him and his club. Does that sound good to you? Does any of it sound good to you?"

The three of them gave that a good twenty count, thinking, and at the end no one actually felt a damn bit better about either scenario or making their decision up. Charlie opened the door slowly, looking left and right. All the offices this time of night were dark. Thank God, he thought. He motioned for the two to follow as if there were any other options. Tim squeezed through behind Charlie and whispered back to Jim, saying, "Don't worry. If you get shot, it'll be okay."

"How the fuck would it be okay if I got shot?"

"No one really likes you. So, it'll be okay, the grief will be short for us."

"Oh, you are just a funny fucker, aren't ya?"

Tim made a kiss noise to Jim, and Charlie snapped at both of them saying, "Quiet game, guys, quiet game. Guess what, you're both fucking failing. Start now."

Jim held up a fist, winding it up and popping a middle finger just for Charlie. When they got to the processing room that led to the lobby, the three raced into the lobby wanting to get out before the desk sergeant could get his lazy ass up and try shooting them. Charlie was actually feeling pretty good about this plan. He actually had not really thought that they would make it this far without getting shot first.

The desk sergeant saw the three of them and obviously looked a bit curious about the fact that they were alone. Even if they were going to cut these guys loose, the jailer would have more than likely kept them in handcuffs until they were processed out and deemed safe to reenter society.

The desk sergeant yelled, "You three-stop, now!"

Mr. Twain walked over, reaching into his inside coat pocket, which Charlie immediately took the wrong way. Charlie only increased his speed, running straight for Mr. Twain, who he could see his eyes were growing visibly more concerned by the moment as he approached, getting nearer and nearer by the second, never slowing down.

Twain dropped the business card holder back in his inside breast pocket, cursing himself for doing so because he realized people were after these three, they probably had a price on their heads.

So, Twain could not blame the guy for being a little on edge, but at the same time was getting too goddamn old for this shit. When they say hits usually hurt worse thinking about them and actually having it happen, they lie. Because, when Charlie ran into him all the air was released from his lungs. Mr. Twain flew backward and hit down on the floor hard, his suit coat flying open, and Charlie reached to take the gun from the inside holster and disarm him and then realized there was no gun to be had.

Charlie asked, "I thought you were going to shoot me?"

Twain held up his index finger needing a minute which didn't take a genius to figure out. He groaned, mumbling, "Why would I shoot you, you idiot?"

"I don't know, because I feel like a lot of people have been trying to shoot me lately."

"Well, I'm not."

"Then what the hell were you grabbing?"

"I was getting a business card that had my name and phone number and information. I was going to give one to each of you, just before you came up and tackled me as hard as you could. You realize that's a very shitty way to introduce yourself to the man who is going to get you out and keep you out of jail right?"

"Oh shit, that's you huh? I take it you know who sent you?"

"Yeah, that's me. Get me up off the goddamn floor. This is a three-thousand-dollar suit, god damn it. You don't look like you can afford to replace too much of my attire. No worries, my employer is happy to make sure that I'm happy."

Charlie went to help him up when Scott, the desk clerk, who probably hadn't had to pull his pistol out of its holster...well in the entire time he'd been a desk sergeant yelled, "Freeze, don't move or I'll shoot!"

Mr. Twain yelled, "You will do no such thing! Holster your weapon and put it away. If you shoot any of these three you are going to have hell to pay, and I'll be representing the Devil. They were not supposed to be in here. You had nothing on them, so theoretically they should never have been here for you to shoot. Wouldn't you agree?"

"Okay, then where the hell is the jailer?"

Charlie cringed a little bit at that saying, "I just thought maybe he'd be more comfortable with the thugs. You know, the ones that you guys put in there to beat us up or kill us, I presume."

Twain looked over, glaring at the officer, "Do you have an explanation for that?"

When the desk sergeant didn't respond, Mr. Twain figured he either did not have a response or didn't have a good one worthy of saying aloud. The desk sergeant finally said, "I need to process them out. But I can't go and leave a goddamn officer in the jail cells."

Jim smiled saying, "Right, but what if the jailer is actually a criminal. Not to try and say that there are any criminals working for the Keys Police Department."

The sergeant looked only to Mr. Twain saying, "Please allow me a minute to go get my coworker."

Twain held up his watch, looking at it, and rolled his finger letting him know that his time was valuable and would not be wasted. As soon as the desk sergeant got out of the main lobby, he was already pulling his phone and calling Detective Lindvall. It only rang twice before Lindvall answered, "Have they been taken care of?"

The desk sergeant replied, "Fuck you, and fuck no, they're not taken care of. Those guys have been nothing but a pain in my goddamn ass. They have been since you brought them here. For God's sake, I don't know what the hell you were thinking? But whatever it was, you were fucking wrong! I thought we'd have the night, but they are already getting out of here."

"What do you mean you are letting them out? Where are you?"

"I'm at the jail, where else would I be? I'm headed back now to get the jailer out. A lawyer showed up and wants them released immediately. I checked with the chief, and he agreed that the charges were bullshit."

"Of course, they are. Where are you getting him out of? What lawyer?"

"A fucking jail cell, what do you think? Where else would he be? It's some guy named Twain."

"I wouldn't ever guess a cell."

The sergeant whistled when he went into the cage hallway for the cells.

Lindvall asked, "What is it now? What do you see?"

"Nothing, just that the six guys that you put in here are probably going to need to go see a doctor."

"I would have thought that six guys would have been enough."

"Oh, it should have been more than enough. From what I can tell there's no shortage of broken noses. Maybe a broken arm. One guy is strapped to a toilet. He's either drowned or passed out. I don't know and quite frankly I don't care."

The jailer saw him and yelled, "Quit fucking looking and get me out of this damn place now!"

"Jesus Christ, you can't even write this shit. What a fucking moron! I'm hanging up, take as long as you can to release them," Lindvall yelled.

It only took a minute for him to get a very pissed-off jailer out of the cell. The desk sergeant hissed saying, "You have no idea how pissed Lindvall is with you."

"What the hell did I do?"

"You had six guys; Lindvall sent you three to be taken care of."

"Yeah, he sent six. I put two in each cell."

"Well, who told you to think?"

"I don't understand."

"Yeah, that's something we've all kind of caught on to. What I mean is, think about it. You could have put all six guys in one cell, kept the other two in the waiting, and then taken them in one by one. There's no way these guys could have taken on six guys at once."

"Okay then, thanks for the lesson on how to ideally put a piece of shit that is probably innocent away."

"Don't get all high and mighty. I'm just saying, don't wreck a good thing."

Charlie and Tim practically lifted Twain up off of the floor. Charlie said, "I really am sorry about that, Mr. Twain."

Twain replied, "Well I've had some crazy experiences in my time. I can take a licking and keep on going. But Mr. Fratto, senior, sent me to collect you and your friends. It seems you've had quite the busy day today."

"Yeah, you could say that" Charlie replied.

"I would also say that chances are Mr. Fratto owes you his life. From the way it sounds, there's something going on tonight, and he is a man whom I do not see get nervous very often."

"No, I would not suspect that he was a man that showed a lot of fear. I would have to figure that it's something he's not really allowed to show."

Mr. Twain finished and got three business cards out saying, "We're going to go somewhere safe. If anything happens and we get split up, you get somewhere safe and you call that number on the card. Day, morning, night, doesn't matter, call it and someone will answer. But if it is something I can't handle which has happened before, but it's been quite rare, then I'll find someone who can."

Charlie whistled saying, "Wow, it's like a real-life JAG lawyer."

Twain had a little gleam in his eye and said, "Yeah, maybe, but I assure you that I can get a hell of a lot angrier. I also don't have quite as many guidelines that I have to deal with."

The jailer came out the door first, heading straight to Charlie. He did not have kindness in his eyes. Charlie wasn't worried about this guy; a fart could blow him over, he thought. The man was screaming, "I'm going to kick your skinny ass, you son of a bitch. Nobody puts me in jail. Goddammit!"

Jim, always the helper, said, "Actually, I think Charlie is a somebody who put you in jail. You don't remember when you put a handcuff on him and then he spun you around and made you go in your own jail? Let me ask you, do you have mental issues or memory issues?"

The man gave a death glare to Jim and went to pull his baton. He'd picked it up on his way back out saying, "I'm going to beat his fucking head open with this thing!"

Just as he was reaching his arm back, Mr. Twain leaned forward in front of Charlie, who was ready to block with a pristine black business card still in his hands. The letters saying Twain Law Firm and Associates stenciled out in silver. The man snapped yelling, "Old man, do you want your goddamn wrist broken? Don't you see what is about to happen?"

"I do, and I did. I would not like to have my wrist broken if it could be at all avoidable. I feel like I've already been hit today an unnecessary number of times. No, what I wanted to say was that

I'm trying to save you a great deal of trouble."

"Yeah? How's that?"

The desk sergeant was trying to do the man a favor, trying to get his attention but he was waving him off as Mr. Twain was growing more irritable with every second that he had to stay inside of this jail. Mr. Twain replied, "Very simple, actually. If you save me the time by not hitting my client with a baton and injuring him or myself, then I won't have to spend weeks and months ensuring your life is completely and utterly ruined. Ponder on that for a few moments and tell me how you feel about it?"

The desk cop, Scott, whispered in his ear, "Do not fuck with this one, that one, or the other."

Scott didn't waste any time. He got around making the paperwork available to sign out releasing them of all charges and any issues relinquishing back the disassembled box of weapons. The sergeant said, "Is there anything else I can do for you tonight, gentlemen?"

Mr. Twain said, "I think that that will be it for tonight."

The jailer who was still fuming said, "What, are you sure you don't want to take our badge numbers? Being the big Billy badass that you are."

Mr. Twain smiled, "783925 and 632154. I do not need to write them down, I have them memorized."

The jailer did not say another word. He could tell that this guy definitely should not be messed with. Mr. Twain looked at his three new clients. He gave them a knowing smile, "I have a feeling with the way this facility is run that chances are I will see you again."

The desk sergeant was going to say something but couldn't think of anything that he would gain by replying to anything. They exited the first set of two doors. Charlie asked, "Is your car close, sir?"

Twain took this the wrong way asking, "Are you hurt? Do you need medical assistance? You're in my care, until Mr. Fratto is able to collect you himself. I assure you if they injured you there'll be a price they can't afford coming after them."

"No, I'm not hurt. Well, no more than I was when I got here. I was just going to ask how far your car is because it is difficult to say if anyone might be out there and waiting for us. I have a feeling some phone calls were probably made while the desk sergeant went to free the jailer."

Being shot wasn't really something that he was overused to. He had gotten into law to be rich, not to be a walking target. Mr. Twain replied, "I'm parked over there in the middle of those two empty spots. I have the Lincoln sedan four-door. Are you wanting me to go get it?"

Charlie said, "As much as I would like to say yes, I don't have the heart to put you in that scenario."

Jim said, "Well, I mean, if he really wants to…"

Charlie nudged Jim with his elbow. He knew he was probably kidding, but… Twain tossed the keys to Charlie saying, "I don't know if I trust this one driving my car."

Charlie looked down at the box of disassembled weapons, really wishing that it wouldn't be so damn awkward looking if he could just reassemble one of the guns here in the lobby. But the longer they stayed there, the more suspicious they were going to look to anyone that was waiting for them in the parking lot. He thought it would probably be ideal if he just got his ass moving and got the four of them the hell out of here.

Charlie did a three-count, shaking his hands to get the nerves out of them. He raced out the doors, not planning to stop until he made it to Twain's car. When red lasers came out of nowhere and started bouncing up and painting the space in front of Charlie, he did not have any feelings of hope or especially safety. Charlie jumped when the concrete in front of him seemed to miraculously disappear. Not that it would have made him feel amazing hearing it, but one additional issue was that Charlie didn't actually hear any gunfire. The sound of the bullets hitting the cement in front of him was louder than anything else he could hear at the moment. Little shrapnel pieces of rock flew up, instantly cutting through to his legs. Charlie could feel new blood trickling down his already bruised legs. Charlie stumbled forward, landing on his hands and knees. He didn't stay down long; staying was death, and death wasn't an option. Charlie made himself get up and dove between a set of cars, trying to think about what his next move should be. He'd never felt so goddamn naked in all of his life. The fact that there were multiple lasers did even less for him.

The lasers seem to be on a mission from God, looking around trying to figure out where he had taken cover under. It took just another moment before the clattering of a steel object bouncing on the ground quickly made him think that whatever was coming his way was worse than the lasers. Charlie had a bad feeling instantly because the hairs on the back of his neck stood up as he realized that was not a good sound at all. He looked down at his feet seeing a small object rolling towards him. Charlie already knew what it was and did not want anything to do with it. He reached down lightning-quick taking it and popped up seeing a man with a rifle and the laser pointing directly towards Charlie, not yet painting him, and Charlie took one massive step back, launching with precision the grenade that he knew had about one to two seconds, at best, left before it would paint Charlie on the two cars he had been trying to hide in between.

The man immediately stopped caring about trying to put the laser sight on Charlie's chest. He knew what the repercussions would be if he stayed where he was. The second shooter, who had been next to him, didn't even take the time to try and register it; he sprinted off running backward and Charlie waited just a moment until the explosion went off and his freedom and chance to get Mr. Twain's car had finally presented itself again.

He wasted no time, knowing that once the wreckage settled, they would be coming back with a vengeance, unless as Charlie prayed that the car flipped over on them. Charlie was hitting the key fob and the automatic start as he raced to Twain's car, leaping in, not treating it quite with the love that he knew the owner probably would have preferred. However, cars could be replaced, lives couldn't.

Charlie hit reverse on the car, punching the gas and propelling himself backward straight towards the three waiting for him in the lobby. He saw Tim, who wasn't a fool, kneeling down, his hands moving through the box like lightning, and when he brought his hands up, he had a pistol in his hand. Normally Charlie wouldn't suggest putting a gun together in the lobby of a police station...but Charlie could see there weren't any police still in the lobby to worry about arresting them...again. Charlie could tell Twain appeared to be giving him legal advice that Tim had probably not requested. All the same though, it was probably still good advice to know. When the grenade had gone off, Jim had looked over his shoulder seeing nothing but an unmanned precinct office. It was pretty apparent to him that whatever happened was not going to be recorded by the Florida Keys Police Department. Jim said, "Can you run, Mr. Twain?"

He shrugged a little saying, "I'm old. I don't really have too many valid reasons to run nowadays. If it's a short run, I'll probably be okay."

Charlie was flying backward in reverse. There was no slowing down until the ass end of the car had almost hit the doors to the precinct. Charlie came to a sliding stop, and when they tried to push out through the door realized that he was too close. Tim and Jim both hit the back bumper of the car trying to exit. Charlie heard it and pulled forward a few feet, giving them the room that they needed to get out. The three ran to the back seat. Jim opened the door, letting Twain in. Tim took the shotgun seat.

Charlie said, "Probably a really good idea that we got out of there. As much as I wanted to worry about them coming in and killing us in our cells, at least now we've got some distance out here to try and put a little space between us and them."

Tim didn't seem to give a shit or think that it was a blessing. He yelled, "This is a really fucked up town. I've never tried to be the popular guy, given our profession and how many drunken sailors we've had to arrest, but Jesus Christ, this is ridiculous. I mean, is there anyone on the Keys besides Mr. Twain here and maybe Fratto who is not trying to kill us?"

Charlie shrugged saying, "I cannot say for sure yes or no."

Jim had the rear light on and was going to town reassembling the shotgun at lightning speed. He was humming a song to himself saying, "I really need to get this gun put together, so the bad guys don't put bullets in my brain. Bullets in my brain. Bullets in my brain, I hope they don't shoot my pecker off."

Charlie wasn't waiting and took the most direct route out of the parking lot that was physically possible. He was pretty confident that issues might arise, but right now and then, he just wanted to get out of this place. The idea of getting somewhere safe was very appealing.

Charlie put everyone into the back of their seat trying to hold on for dear life as he flew down the parking lot. One of the two men came out, switching the gun to full auto, Charlie assumed, and unleashed hell on the front of the car. All he managed to do was to hit the right headlight and seem to mistake the cards with which he was currently holding.

Charlie hated just about everything about this, so when he raced across the parking lot and the dipshit was in his way, Charlie absolutely without an ounce of remorse did not swerve or let off the pedal. He went straight at the man. The guy realized at the last second, he wasn't stopping or worrying about his well-being. The gunman jumped and Charlie hit him going forty just under his waist, taking his feet out from beneath him. Charlie only pressed harder on the gas, sending him onto the hood to the windshield, making it spiderweb before finally bouncing once hard off the roof and onto the concrete behind them. He had pretty shitty control over his trigger finger and let off a slew of shots. Charlie smiled saying, "God damn that felt good. Motherfucker trying to shoot me. I wish they both would have come out in front of your car."

Twain gave Charlie his address to plug into the GPS, and they headed in that direction. He said, "Yes, you know some people might think a Lincoln Continental might just be one of those cars that you treat with a little respect. I guess that doesn't apply to you, does it?"

"Yeah, sorry about that, do you have insurance?"

"Just go to that address, Mr. Ford."

Jim, not helping, said, "Hey, the inside of this thing is pretty nice, Mr. Twain."

Chapter 9

Fratto Junior had been sitting by his phone all day. He knew that this thing had to go down precisely perfectly and without question or the repercussions for it quite literally would be deadly. He'd been waiting for that damn call, and it just seemed to keep not coming. After he had almost given up on ever hearing from anyone a knock came at the door. He yelled, "Damn it! I know that you guys know I'm busy tonight?"

Detective Lindvall opened the door, and he made his way in. Lindvall didn't ask to sit. He didn't have the power that Fratto had or that junior could have if he was able to accomplish this feat. But what he did have was the ability to arrest and kill people. Both of these things were ideal for a man who pushed the line when it came to the law, and by push it would probably resemble a pretzel upon further review. Junior asked, "So, do you have good news for me?"

The detective wasn't a kiss ass; he didn't necessarily go out of his way to try and be on everyone and their mother's good sides. So, he answered honestly, "No, everything has not been going as planned. Your two guys that tried to drown Ford fucked up. I'm pretty sure tonight Nydegger gave up all the information on you. Your dad probably knows what's going on by now. If he's still alive, I don't want to imagine the repercussions for you and your crew. Oh, and the three that I put in jail, one of them being Ford, the three of them are already out. I had sent two gunmen ahead of me to take care of them, locked and loaded with machine guns and grenades with no interference from anyone inside the precinct. Guess what, they fucked up too."

"Do you have any good news?"

"Yeah, I haven't gotten shot tonight. I'd say that as you try to develop your empire, that I think you might want to begin considering just on the off chance that you want to live to see thirty, that you need to learn that you get what you pay for."

"What is it that I'm buying that's cheap?"

"Help, your help, they have to be cheap. Otherwise, they're fucking you over and still not delivering on what it is that you want done. As of right now, I don't think anything good has happened or gone as expected for you."

Junior knew his dad and his temper. It was where he got his own from. However, he had seen his dad upset before. It was not a good thing; it took some people time to get used to inflicting pain on others. However, this was in no way the same case for Fratto. It was a dangerous goddamn world and there were plenty of sharks in it. Fratto was absolutely not prey. If there was an alpha in the Keys, he was definitely one of them.

Junior ran his hands through his long black hair that went all the way down to his shoulders. He knew it wouldn't help but still felt like he wanted to rip it from his scalp. He yelled, "I can't believe all this planning, and nothing is going as it was supposed to. What in the fuck? God damn it, does dad know for sure?"

Lindvall shrugged saying, "I've been trying to clean shit up all day for you. But there's just a trail of it and it doesn't seem like it's getting any thinner."

Fratto opened up his desk drawer, pulling out two different Glocks that had been modified illegally to fire off fully automatic. He looked at each pistol, making sure neither had their safeties on and the extended magazines were both full. All he wanted to do was know that if someone came to that door who was uninvited that they would be met with no shortage of lead. Junior was trying to be cocky and said, "Yeah, let my dad try and come here. He'll see what's up."

Lindvall didn't feel like poking the beehive. If he needed to lie to himself to feel tough or safe, then that was fine by him. Lindvall smiled a noncommittal type, not really filling Junior with a hell of a lot of feelings that Lindvall thought that success was going to happen for him. He got up saying, "Well at least you know when they arrive if they, or when they, come for you."

"How's that?"

"You aren't the only one in town who has automatics. Your dad doesn't skimp, and if someone doesn't do what they are supposed to for him, then that is the end of them. Second chances aren't a thing; forgiveness means weakness, especially in your family's line of work."

"So, what, I should go and kill everyone that screwed the pooch tonight?"

Lindvall shrugged. He wasn't a crime boss in the Keys and didn't want to be. He'd carved himself out a wonderful niche in his world and didn't have any interests in fucking that up. Lindvall said, "I think that I'll keep my opinions to myself and head out."

"You know if you could stay for the night, I can pay you a stack of my favorite presidents. Sound good?"

"You know, any other time it would, but I think I'm going to need to pass tonight."

"You don't like money?"

Lindvall was already at the door. He twisted the knob before saying, "Dead men don't spend money. Keep your eyes open, Junior. I'll reach out once the dust settles."

"Your loss."

Lindvall waved politely, heading out, not too worried about the rest of his evening.

Chapter 10

Fratto didn't care for waiting, but unfortunately, he didn't have a choice. The options available were slim at the moment. He wanted to make sure everything was safe before he made a move. Phil pulled up next to Fratto's car, or what was left of it. Fratto waited, wanting to make sure there wasn't anything lacking in Phil's loyalty. Phil got out of the car, walking up to the window and knocking on the blacked-out driver's window. Fratto watched, and when he didn't pull a gun and fire through the window, he came out of the shadows, letting the hammer on his pistol go back into its place. Phil jumped a foot when he heard the hammer go back. He knew working with Fratto had its perks but there was absolutely no shortage of dangers that came with the territory.

Phil grabbed his heart, trying to make sure he wasn't having a heart attack. He whispered, "Christ, Mr. Fratto you trying to give me a heart attack? Why aren't you in the car?"

"Because you don't live in a business like this by taking stupid chances. You came alone, though?"

"Isn't that what you asked me to do, sir?"

"Yeah, that's correct, what'd you bring?"

Phil walked to the rear of his SUV, opening up the rising hatch. "Well, I didn't think you'd want me to waste any time, so I got what I could from one of the storage units."

Fratto saw a small armory in front of him and felt some relief from the fact that he had stash houses and spots around town. The ability to get what he needed at any time didn't break his heart. There was something to say about being prepared. Fratto smiled, he loved American-made items. But tonight, he was just fine with a beautiful blacked-out Belgian machine gun. He liked them because they took NATO rounds, and if shit hit the fan, they'd be able to find ammunition anywhere. There were drum magazines for it and Fratto took a duffel bag worth of them. If he ran out of ammunition it would be because he should have never begun shooting in the first place.

Phil asked, "What's the plan, Mr. Fratto?"

He had been thinking of the same thing. Normally, he didn't rush into shit, planning and making sure he did things right was the smart play. It was also the reason he'd lived so long in a world where old men weren't a thing. Unfortunately, he knew that if he wasted too much time that he wouldn't have to worry about making a plan because they'd come to him, and if they weren't ready, he'd be murdered.

A slew of headlights came on. Fratto was instantly thinking that he needed to bury a bullet in Phil's brain. Whether that reason be for incompetence or betrayal was yet to be seen. Right now, though the numbers would be thoroughly against him if he took action. Phil saw the headlights and said, "Damn it, there must be a tracker on the SUV or car."

"Yeah, I was hoping that was the case."

"I'm one hundred percent in, sir. You know that I wouldn't do anything against you...ever."

"Good. If I were you, I'd grab a gun."

Phil didn't hesitate, knowing exactly what he had placed in the rear of his vehicle. He asked, "Can I ask what in the hell is going on, sir?"

"It's Junior."

"Did something happen to him, is he alright?"

"No, he isn't alright. He lost his fucking mind."

It took Phil a second to realize or think he realized what he was saying. Phil asked as honestly as he could, "I'm sorry, sir, but are you trying to say that all these guns are for your son?"

Fratto held up his carry pistol. He said, "Oh no, this is for my son. These are for all the guys that have the balls to stand in my way and to try and take what is mine and what will always be mine for as long as I god damn want it!"

"I'm sorry to..."

"Save it, you see those headlights, well they aren't with us so they must be against us. I need you to rain down on them with hell's fire."

Phil set the machine gun back down. It took Fratto a moment to figure out what the hell he was doing. Phil had this thing set up like his life depended on it. He politely scooted Fratto out of the way and undid a metal latch. Fratto was going to ask what in the hell he was doing. He didn't need to because Phil wasn't seeing wasting any time. When he saw the cars were in the distance but had begun moving and were nearing them quickly, Phil tried to put himself into a faster-moving gear. He wanted to be ready, live, and most importantly not let Fratto senior down.

Fratto watched, thinking something was completely wrong apparently. He wasn't quite sure what to expect but at the same time was definitely second-guessing himself trying to figure out what it was. Phil pulled out a large rectangular box that was three to four feet long and a few feet wide. He thought the box was something that he was going to open to get something out of. Fratto of course could not have guessed any more incorrectly.

Phil pulled the box all the way out until it couldn't go any further and clicked into place. It released a bipod that fell down off of the bottom of it to support what Fratto figured had to be a pretty decent amount of weight given the size of the box. Phil flipped two switches on the side and a spring came up that was mounted under a gun that Fratto had never seen before but instantly fell in love with. It had a set of laser sights on it that turned on immediately and a single trigger to send a rain of hell down on anything in its path.

Phil smiled a little, pulling back the charge handle mechanism to make sure there was a round ready to roll in the chamber. Phil painted the laser onto the approaching vehicle and pulled the trigger back sending off thousands upon thousands of rounds of ammunition directly towards the vehicles who merely seconds before thought that they had the upper hand. They couldn't have been more wrong if they'd have tried.

The bullet casings rained down dancing off the dark pavement below. Fratto recognized the 5.56 rounds, smiling, and the oncoming approaching vehicles did not have a chance to get within 200 yards of them. They also didn't have the opportunity to fire. Phil did not so much as let off of the trigger for a millisecond. He held that trigger down, sending the majority of the rounds through the windshields of each car. He was pretty confident he had hit home with what he was aiming at when the vehicles collided into each other, coming to a quick and violent stop. Fratto still had his Belgian machine gun in his hand ready to fire the rifle but at the same time did not think that there was going to be much need for that to be done. Fratto looked down at the ground and there was an impossible amount of bullet casings painting the cement around his feet. It basically looked like Rambo had come in to save the day in the Keys.

Phil let off the trigger and the only downside was that neither of them currently could hear a goddamn thing. Phil looked at Fratto yelling because he knew if he was deaf that his boss probably was too saying, "I think that took care of the son of a bitches!"

Fratto had somewhat understood just by the mouthing of the words. He realized that he now had a brand-new favorite gun. He thought installing one of these in the rear of all of his cars might be for the greater good. Well, he thought at least his greater good and ultimate survival which of course was typically the priority.

Fratto walked over to his car doing something on the inside before coming back out, tossing a flare into the back seat of his car. The two drove off with a fireball erupting behind them. Fratto was a pro and had always been quite smart when it came to making sure he didn't leave any evidence or prints behind. Phil asked, "Where do you want to go now, sir?"

Fratto pointed back towards the Keys saying, "I think it's probably time that I go see Junior. The next few days are probably going to be bloody. So, just remember who you work for, and we'll make it through this."

"I never had any doubt who I should work for, sir. You point out who to shoot; that's fine with me, Mr. Fratto."

Fratto said, "Head over to poker night. We're going to pick up the rest of the boys, every single person that I've seen tonight is somebody that's not on my crew, with the exception of that new driver. We're going to have a little bit harder hiring process in the future of finding the one who chauffeurs me around. If I can't trust the guy driving me, then who the hell can I trust?"

Phil gunned the engine, knowing time was of the essence. Fratto hit the speed dial, trying to keep some of his composure. He wasn't necessarily known as being someone who had a personality that dealt with people who disrespected him in any way whatsoever. It answered on the second ring. The gruff voice said, "You got Mikey's place. What can I do ya for?"

Fratto replied, "Sounds like you didn't pick the right side, Mikey."

Mikey's balls went up into his throat. Mikey wasn't sure if he was going to puke. He definitely felt like if his balls didn't go into his throat then someone had kicked them. When he realized he was talking to Fratto senior, everything that was supposed to have happened apparently had not. He hadn't figured that things had gone amazingly well given the fact that no one had come back from their designated jobs which they were supposed to take care of before they came back. He thought that Fratto's voice would be the last one he would hear, again.

Mikey replied already knowing the answer, saying, "Mr. Fratto, is that you, sir?"

Fratto said, "You sound like you are talking to a ghost, Mikey. Haven't I always been good to you? Did I ever do anything bad by you, Mikey?"

"No, no sir, not once, you've always been good to me, sir."

"Then why in the fuck are you answering the phone acting like my own blood didn't just try and have me killed more than once today. Were you that god damn confident in Junior that you wanted to take that chance? That, that was the card you decided to play?"

"He didn't give me a choice, sir. He said if I didn't do what he wanted that he was going to kill me. I haven't really had any play in it. I've just been here working tonight."

Fratto couldn't hold back the laugh and replied, "And what the fuck do you think I'm gonna do? If you're still there when we arrive, I'm going to take care of every single person in that bar personally. No guns, no knives, it's going to be baseball bats, crowbars, and pliers. We will be rewriting the definition of pain, and I assure you it is going to be anything but pleasant. Do you understand me?"

Mikey said, "Without any doubt, sir. Would you like to talk to anyone else in the establishment tonight before I leave?"

Fratto wanted to make sure he had the point and asked, "Am I gonna ever see you again, Mikey?"

"No sir, never."

"Good, now go give the phone to Junior. Don't take this notice as any kind of reason to think that I'm being generous. Don't think that I will give you any leeway if you are still there when I show up. If you are still in Florida when the sun comes up, you are fucking dead."

"You'll never see me again, sir. The United States is damn big. I'm confident that I can go to many other places."

"See that you do, Mikey. See that you do."

Mikey replied, "Hold on. Just a moment, please. I'll take the phone to Junior myself."

"Oh, I know you will, Mikey. You might find a new career. I don't think criminal activity is good for you."

Mikey didn't answer; he knew Fratto senior was right, and he wasn't going to get anywhere further with the man by continuing talking to him. He'd basically thrown him a lifeline from this, and he wasn't going to waste it. Mikey opened the door without knocking. Junior had his guns both up and aiming. He fired off a slew of shots, not hesitating. Mikey stumbled forward, falling to his knees, trying to grip onto wherever hurt worse at the moment. Unfortunately, the competition of pain was too great, and he just began to bleed out. Junior didn't feel great about this; he knew he'd need as many people as he could to help keep this place as safe as possible.

Junior waved to the men outside, "Everything is alright. I'd suggest you knock, though, if you need something. Tonight isn't the night for surprises. Someone come and get Mikey and take him out of here, now."

The men shut Junior's door. Junior got up, looking down and seeing the house phone on the floor. He picked it up, seeing that the time on call was still going. He wasn't sure what to say or if there was anyone still there. Junior answered, "Who is this?"

"You know I would say that I am disappointed in you…but I've never been too proud of you in the first place. I hope you felt like a big man today…because you couldn't have fucked up worse."

"Dad?"

"Who the hell do you think it is?"

"Damn it, I just shot Mikey for coming into my office."

"He should have knocked, I guess. Don't worry. You will see him again soon."

"He's dead."

"You never were a smart kid. I don't understand it; your mom wasn't stupid, and I sure as hell am not either. Maybe you hit your head too many times. Otherwise, all that shit you put up your nose might have been behind it. If you'd have listened a little more, we might not be where we are tonight."

"The night is still young. I don't think you can say for sure how things are going to end, Dad."

"Oh, I think that I can make a pretty accurate guess. You wanted power, and I can appreciate that. But you went after it in the wrong way. I don't think you had a goal that you could achieve."

"You didn't seem like you were retiring anytime soon. So, I was going to help you make up your mind."

"There's a difference in being retired and murdered, you dumb son of a bitch. I'll help you realize that when I get there."

"You think that's a good idea, pops...coming here?"

"Well, I guess that is yet to be seen, isn't it?"

"I'll be waiting for you, pops."

"I hope that you do, but if you aren't there when I show up then you can sleep with one eye open for the rest of your life...what's left of it at least."

Junior was going to start to say something else when the house phone gave a dial tone. Junior set the phone down and knew that he should keep a good head on his shoulders tonight. Unfortunately, the demons that haunted him were like a scratching under his skin trying to get out...one which he could not fix any other way. Junior pulled a vial out of his pocket, spinning the top off and tapping it onto his desk until a pile that would temporarily fix his itch sat in front of him. He always told himself today was the last day...but today was never the right one to be done.

Chapter 11

Bruno and Lou had been minutes away from the boat being fully submerged in the water. Neither was a strong swimmer and after Charlie had done a pretty good job of kicking their asses it made it that much more difficult to try and think about having to stay afloat. There were life preservers in the boat, but they knew either way they were never going to hear the end of this from whoever picked them up. They also knew that they'd owe their saviors big time, or at least that's what they had thought until the boat came up flashing its lights to let them know they were there.

Sid had a rope in his hands and tossed it to the two so they could tie off and get on board. Sid made the instant mistake of saying, "Wow, did you guys fuck up. Nydegger is fucking pissed, everything's gone to shit tonight. Junior ain't too happy with nobody...but he's losing people so fast that he can't take anyone out who is fucking up on account that there aren't enough people."

Bruno climbed across first. Bruno knew that the boat wasn't gonna go down any faster with only having Lou on board. Sid said, "You two are on Junior's shit list. You know you're probably going to be lucky if you..."

Bruno brought a Goliath-sized hand back before Sid could contemplate reacting. He didn't hold anything back when he punched him, aiming, and connecting squarely in his face. The recent work the local mob doctor had done resetting his face on his previously broken nose had just been undone.

Sid went to reach for his nose when Bruno was already throwing a second punch directly into his throat. Minty was watching this from the driver's seat, not really loving the idea of everything currently happening. He knew they had not been flawless in their execution of what they had been tasked with to do. Sid was fighting for air, coughing, holding his nose and throat. Bruno pulled out a pistol, putting it up next to his head. Lou jumped over onto the boat trying to deescalate saying, "Bruno, relax, take it easy okay, please?"

Bruno spoke as smoothly and cool as possible, "Give me one goddamn reason why I shouldn't murder this son of a bitch right here and make sure that he never has the chance to fuck up again?"

"Because, and only because as he just said, there's not enough guys currently to go around. What we need to do is survive the night. When we get back to shore, I promise that finding those three is going to be top on my list of things to do."

Bruno looked down at Sid, whose eyes were streaming, and he said, "Don't mention anything about us fucking up anymore, Sid. Because if you do then realize that dead men can't pick up people in the middle of the damn ocean. If you guys would have done your job correctly, then we would have been able to circle back around, get Charlie and take his ass out."

Sid nodded, barely able to see a blurry Bruno through his tear-filled eyes. Lou let out a sigh of relief. He didn't want to have to worry about the odds being stacked against them any more than they already were. He did know that if it was the last thing he did, which given the circumstances he thought it might be, that he was going to kill Charlie Ford and his two friends. Lou yelled, "Hey Minty, get this thing in gear and get us back to the shore. Sid, go clean yourself up."

Sid didn't say anything about how they looked. Minty didn't even so much as give a thumbs up. He put the boat in gear, holding back just a hair, not wanting to throw Bruno off balance. Minty wasn't stupid; he knew he was probably on his shit list as well. It would not improve until these issues had been rectified. The four of them raced back to the shore, not wasting any time doing so. This night seemed to be the one which would not end anytime soon. All anyone on the boat wanted at the moment was to survive this night.

When they got to the docks and secured the boat, the four wasted no time heading out. Minty and Sid had done one thing right, and that was making sure there was no shortage of firearms and a replenishment of ammunition. Bruno said, "Do we know where they are?"

"Who, Bruno?" Minty asked a little scared to get the answer.

"The assholes that should have been dead by now."

"There's a few of them, you know…I mean that should have…"

"Christ, Ford and his two thugs, that's who. Where the hell are they?"

"Junior said that they got put in jail but got right out. Lindvall didn't have the charges they needed to hold them so they could keep them in jail."

"I thought Lindvall had the guys who could be in there to take care of people."

"Bruno, I don't know, I'm just telling you what information I got. I really don't know where they are or how to find them. I've been spending the last few hours going to pick your asses up."

"Okay, Minty, Bruno, relax, alright? It has been a long, shitty day. If we can get through this, then the day is over."

Bruno was thinking about the day being over. He was also remembering the words of Nydegger who he wasn't scared of but knew he did have things at his disposal mostly because he knew that Junior had been trying to keep things on the down-low about what he was doing. Unfortunately, though, everything had gotten out of hand and wasn't looking any better. When the day had begun there'd been pretty high hopes that they'd be climbing up the food chain in the Keys. But right now, it didn't seem like they would survive the day or at all.

Bruno said, "Then why don't we go for a drive and see if we can find them. I know it seems like a big city, but it really isn't all that big. We know pretty god damn well where they won't be, so that just leaves where they might be."

The common sense and the stupidity wrapped into that was almost hard to take seriously. Lou thought it was about as smart as when someone told him that he'd always find something in the last place he looked when he finally found it. Bruno he knew was riding on the edge tonight and he didn't want to get murdered just because he brought up how stupid what Bruno was saying was, so he didn't. Sid said, "I'm not gonna try no more bombs. I get a eye on those fuckers and all I'm going to do is empty my magazine on them. If we see Fratto senior driving around, do you think we should take care of that for Junior?"

Lou said, "I think if we see either of them that it'd be a wise idea to take them out. It might be an opportunity that we don't want to pass up and if we did then we probably wouldn't want to mention that to anyone."

Chapter 12

Charlie wasn't necessarily a violent person, but he wasn't scared to fight, or to make things even. He wasn't having any remorse about Mr. Twain's car at the moment. He knew that if Fratto lived, he would handsomely take care of Mr. Twain. He was looking at the old man in the backseat. If there was something on his mind, he wasn't giving any signs of it. He'd seen some cool characters, but this one topped the cake. Charlie asked, "So, if you wouldn't mind, Mr. Twain, I was doing some thinking…"

Twain interrupted him saying, "Look Mr. Ford…"

"Charlie, just call me Charlie, please."

"Listen Mr. Ford, I'm here for business, that's it. We don't need to be friends; we are business associates and that is all that I would like to be. Do you understand what I am saying to you? You know that nine out of ten times when someone starts off a sentence with the fact that they were thinking that it usually leads to nothing good. In fact, that's how I've gotten a good majority of clients from men and women, mind you, who wanted to be the smartest one in the room. The thinker, the planner, the one big job getter, well, that isn't the case, see. You need to come with me to this safe house and wait. Is that really that difficult?"

""Unfortunately, I don't know if I am able to do that."

"You don't know if you are able to follow the easiest of directions.

Is that what you are attempting to tell me?”

“Yes, sir. That is exactly what I am saying.”

“Why?”

“We have client confidentiality, right?”

“From the minute I went into that police station, you and I had an understanding, son. Nothing you say or do can be discussed with anyone. There isn’t anything anyone can do to make me speak. I assure you; I’ve dealt with tougher cops than the ones in this precinct before. I didn’t get where I am today by backing down.”

“Okay good. I don’t know how many of the lower life types you know in the Keys or if you are just mostly working solely for Fratto, but his goons killed my uncle. I’m going to rectify that tonight. I won’t bore you with the details.”

“You’ve already used a gun tonight I assume?”

“Yes.”

“Then even the smallest amount of gun residue is going to be on your skin. Might I suggest that you try and figure out an alternative measure to firearms. If you are tied to their murders, then it would be very difficult to try and get you off. Life is full of chances, but second chances are not as plentiful.”

Charlie was tapping his fingers on the steering wheel. He hadn't really thought about how he was going to kill them. Just that death was his end goal. Tim said, "Thank you, Mr. Twain, I am confident that we will have much greater success this time."

Charlie didn't say anything but thought a boat ride wasn't out of the question just yet. He wouldn't be a stupid shopper when it came to purchasing supplies. There'd be no shortage when it came to picking the cement with the quickest drying time. Charlie was still truly contemplating vigilante justice. He didn't want other people to take care of his problems, but at the same time didn't want to have these guys haunting his dreams. If he was lucky, he could kill them in self-defense. His hatred for them was strong, but Charlie could only imagine that they would be just as excited to see the three of them after leaving them on the boat in the middle of nowhere.

"I am sure that you will; just be careful."

Charlie took Mr. Twain home. He'd assured the men that there was no sense in just him going to a safe house. He was more than confident that his home would be just fine and safe. There'd be no issues with anyone if they tried to get into his house. There'd been no skimping at any time with his home's design. He'd been under Fratto's employment during construction and had spared nothing when it came to the home's safety and security. Charlie pulled up to a house that definitely said there was money inside. However, there was definitely some money put into the home which would keep those uninvited from entering. Charlie said,

"Can I ask one favor, Mr. Twain?"

"You can ask, yes."

Charlie wasn't used to people like Mr. Twain. He didn't spend this much time around people with such manners. He asked, "Can you tell me where we might find Junior?"

"Mr. Ford, if Mr. Fratto had already expressed interest in taking care of his own son, then I would highly suggest you do not pursue that issue. You see, if he thinks that you are disrespecting him, I would fear that you will get no second chances with Mr. Fratto. He does not stand for any sort of insubordination."

"I won't lay a hand on him. I want to find Bruno and Lou and their two dipshits that work with them. See, if we can find them, then I can put everything else into motion...just as soon as I figure out what's next."

Jim couldn't help himself...or he could but decided against it. He said, "So the plan at the moment is to go to Junior's place. Then we see if the guys you want to kill are there, and if they are, that's when we decide on a plan to come up with? Are you forgetting that the four of them had tried with a zero amount of success to kill the three of us? I mean, if they'd have bought a better cement bag then there's zero chance that Tim would have been able to find you. You'd just be a future part of a coral reef."

"I don't think that reefs work like that, Jim."

"Oh, I'm sorry you're right, because it'll matter when you're dead and drowned in the water or shot and in the water. I mean, either way it isn't going to seem nearly as important to you once that happens. I mean, I guess you could be pissed-off in heaven, given that's where you're going."

Tim hated agreeing with Jim almost ninety-nine percent of the time. However, today he did agree with him. It was not preferable, but it was inevitable at times. Tim nodded saying, "You know I don't like saying when he's right. But I also don't want to see any of you guys or myself getting hurt, blown up, or drowned, et cetera."

Mr. Twain bent down looking through Tim's window and said, "If I might give you one last piece of advice this evening, Mr. Ford?"

Charlie nodded his head saying, "Yeah sure."

"Just remember, it isn't always the revenge that you're hoping for. When you get it but sometimes it's an entirely different kind of monster that you must deal with. Does that make sense to you, Mr. Ford?"

Charlie wasn't actually a hundred percent sure that he did understand what he was saying and questioned him, asking, "So, you don't actually think we should take those guys out?"

Mr. Twain tapped on Tim's door saying, "I'm just giving you some free advice, Mr. Ford. Unlike the men that you wish to go after, there is a certain moral code that good people tend to live by. I would like to think that you are one of those types, as well. I feel just as confident that if you did follow through with whatever you are contemplating doing that your demons very well might just show up to haunt you."

Charlie didn't know how he could let them live and then stay in the same town. It didn't seem like it would be a match made in heaven and they also didn't scream letting bygones be bygones. But demons were not something which he needed in his mindset. Charlie had had plenty of times that the horrific nightmare of his last moments spent with his mother and father rolling down those rocks did not leave him aching for more nightmares to add to his dreams.

Mr. Twain handed him the address to Junior's place and said over his shoulder, "If you should need my services again tonight, do not hesitate to call. I do enjoy my sleep, but when working for Mr. Fratto, it is not always the best job for someone who needs to rest on a regular basis. Luckily though...it affords me the ability to get the best bed and sheets which money can buy."

Charlie put the car in gear and headed straight for Junior's club, hoping very much that he would be able to find Bruno and Lou and put an end to this once and for all. He did appreciate Mr. Twain's advice but knew very well that if things went badly that he would have no qualms about killing the four of them. Because he had a feeling that they would shoot first and ask questions later as well. Which, of course, would lead them to making bad decisions.

Jim asked, "So, at some point, we are going to come up with a plan, correct?"

Charlie replied, "Yes, that seems like it would probably be the intelligent thing to do, Jim. I appreciate your insight. Do either of you have any ideas of what we could actually do to get these fucks out of our lives and not need to look over our shoulder for the rest of our lives? Of course, that is assuming today's not our last day on Earth."

Tim shook his head saying, "Damn, Charlie, you really know how to sell an idea. Come down to the Keys, help me out, guys. Hey, maybe if we're lucky, people will try and blow us up, shoot us, and the only time you'll get to take a dip in the ocean is when a bomb blast forces you into it or your friend is drowning with cement on his legs and needs a big strong man to come save his ass."

"Guys, the minute this is done, there is no expense on the liquor that I am going to purchase for us at whichever club you guys want to go to. I will make sure and tell every woman there that she will not find a man more chivalrous than the two of you."

They headed straight for the club, not stopping for anything along the way.

Chapter 13

Fratto and Phil had not wasted any time other than going directly to the poker night and picking up a crew of five loyal men. The ones that Fratto senior didn't have to question. He knew how committed to him they were when he had not been overly revealing about what they were doing and why they were doing it. Phil waited until it was just the two of them before asking, "So, what's the plan then?"

Fratto said, "I say we pull up on the building, turn the brights on, all except for ours. I want to back it in and I'm going to paint everything seven foot up with a bullet. I won't stop until the building looks like it's going to collapse."

"I thought maybe you would want to shoot a little lower, sir?"

"I would if I wanted to kill anyone. However, what I want is for the son of a bitches to come outside groveling on their hands and knees like little bitches praying that I don't murder them."

"What if someone innocent is inside of the bar?"

"Then I'm going to call bullshit on the fact that they're innocent. Tourists don't go there, and anyone in town knows to stay out of there unless they're invited. So, especially this late at night, there's an even slimmer chance that there are going to be a lot of patrons hanging out in there."

Phil was nodding his head, not a hundred percent sure he agreed. But the logic that he used did seem to make sense. He finally replied, "We can do whatever you want, sir. If I can stay by your side tonight, I think that might be best."

Phil asked, "What do you want the rest of the boys to do?"

"You can have them shoot anyone that comes out, in the arms, hands, legs, hell even the ass but not the chest or head. By the time tonight is over, I'm never going to be disrespected again. I feel like it will get my point across perfectly."

"Well, let me just tell you that I'm glad I'm not on your bad side, sir. If you don't mind me saying, if Junior was a little smarter he might be a little more worried about what's coming for him."

"Unfortunately, I'm not quite sure where I went wrong with him. But obviously something didn't work out in his head."

"I've known some pretty smart people, Mr. Fratto, and they've had some seriously dumbass kids. I've never understood it myself. At this age, I don't necessarily have to worry about it. I mean, with the exception of having to worry about tonight."

"Tonight's gonna go off without a hitch. Stick by my side, and it'll take care of itself."

Phil couldn't say that he was a hundred percent sure that things would go so smoothly, but he knew his boss would die trying. The squad of vehicles pulled into the gravel parking lot. Fratto knew a coward would run out the back. So, he ordered two of them to go to the rear and Fratto and two others took the front. Phil backed in and the other two parked, angling their brights on the building. They got the machine gun mounted and set and Fratto hit his radio, asking, "Is everyone in place?"

Four affirmatives came back and Fratto said, "You guys might get behind your doors for just a minute in the back. I don't know how tough this building is. It might not be tough enough to stop the rounds coming at it."

Fratto gave it a good ten count, looking down at the fully stocked gun and squeezing the trigger, unleashing hell on anything in its path. Junior was sitting at his desk, basically trying to formulate a plan. One which, preferably for him, would not end up leading ultimately to his death. There was nothing about today which was going to be pleasant, but if he could at least figure out how to take out his dad, then unless one of his men stepped up he would be in charge with no one protesting. A knock came at the door, Billy stuck his head through the door yelling, "Don't shoot, don't shoot! It's Billy, relax."

Junior was rubbing his finger on the desk, getting the last bits of powder off of it and rubbing it on his gums. He wasn't really hurting for money, but like any addict he did not want to waste any of what he considered to be precious. He snapped, "What the hell do you want, Billy? Can't you see I'm busy?"

Billy could see the sweat on his boss's brow, his pupils dilated, and his eyes both looking bloodshot yet at the exact same time were the size of cue balls. He replied, "Yes sir, Junior. I know exactly that you're a busy man. I'm sorry to interrupt you, I just thought you should know…"

Junior, never necessarily known for being a patient man, slammed his hand on his desk yelling, "Just get to it, Billy. Things aren't going amazing tonight. Are you sure that you think delivering bad news is a good idea?"

He shrugged, "I don't think that I have a choice. If you prefer, I can leave, but I just thought you'd probably want to know."

"Know what?"

"It's your dad."

"What in the hell does that mean?"

"No, it's your dad. He's outside."

Junior knew that this would be the end-all for tonight. It was either going to go one way or the other, and he knew the only way his dad was going to leave would be with him and all of his crew dead or in body bags. Junior tried playing it cool, but it wasn't necessarily the easiest of things to do. Junior hit the intercom that was wired into the entire building yelling, "Everybody, everybody now! Get your guns, make sure you're loaded. Hell's on its way here. I don't know if they're gonna come in or just shoot from the outside."

Everyone stupidly got up on barstools looking out the rectangle windows that surrounded the building. They added an extra three feet to their height. If they were smarter, then they would have realized that was not going to be an ideal thing.

Junior's heart skipped a beat when the gunfire began. The sound was deafening, and it didn't take a genius to know some sort of machine gun was being used and they were not worried whatsoever, about running out of bullets. He began to wonder if the gunfire would ever cease. Junior being the badass 'wannabe' mob boss that he was, grabbed both pistols and hit the floor. He was not a skinny man, and his army crawl left something to be desired.

He made his way up to the door that led out into the bar where all of his men were. The idea of having an assurance of strength in numbers and not being all alone seemed important at the moment. The glass from the windows was shattering by the second as well. There was a constant shower of drywall, brick, and whatever else this old ass building had been made from. He was getting more pissed by the moment but when he looked up seeing that his men were standing on stools as the gunfire was erupting none of them seemed to have the common sense to realize the shooter was aiming high. Junior was thinking of the old children's tale of the cat that died from curiosity and couldn't think of a better way to put it.

He watched as all of his best men (well, the men that were stupid enough to go against his father) had their heads practically cut through the middle and Junior had to watch their lifeless bodies falling to the ground, landing in impossible positions that they'd never be capable of alive. He did not feel a great deal of hope at this moment. He really just wanted these rounds to stop pelting the building or tearing through it with a vengeance that almost made it seem like the bullets had a personal vendetta as well, even though Junior was quite confident it was just the rage that his father was more than happy to show.

Junior looked around realizing a sobering shitty fact that the bullets cutting his building to pieces had all but taken out all of his men; anyone left probably would bleed out in a matter of minutes. Junior felt like the gunfire was never going to end. However, he was wrong. The gunfire finally did stop, and it didn't actually make him feel all that much better, because it meant his dad would be coming next. His dad was the boogeyman and a nightmare all rolled into one sadistic, relentless, unsympathetic Italian.

Junior stared down at his pistols, thinking it would probably be the best opportunity he would have to go out painlessly. He didn't know if it was the drugs or if he was just too stupid to make a good decision but for some reason he still felt like maybe, just maybe, he had a chance to come out on top. Junior kept thinking if he just waited long enough, eventually they would come in to finish off any poor bastard still there. It would be at that time, he thought that maybe it would be his chance...his only chance to rectify what had been very well one of the worst days of his goddamn life.

Junior lay there, waiting patiently until the inevitable happened and his dad's crew or a handful of them came in, weapons drawn and ready to clean up whatever was left. Junior watched their faces, realizing they had expected someone...anyone...to still be alive. The crew had probably not anticipated the men choosing death by stupidity. Any sensible and intelligent person he thought would have gotten off the chairs the minute they saw whatever that insane gun was. Junior knew damn well that if he'd have seen it he would have stayed as low to the ground as his fat ass would have let him. He recognized the men because he'd known them for years. One of them whispered, "Fratto is gonna be pissed. These guys were supposed to be alive. What the hell are we gonna tell him?"

"You don't tell him a goddamn thing. He can come in here and see that everyone was taken out with his own eyes."

The two men stood post inside the door, waiting patiently, and hoping that he would not take it out on them. They couldn't see how the blame could fall at their feet given the fact that he was the one firing the gun in the first place.

Fratto came in. His son knew his dad had a love for firearms. He always used the comparison of living in New York where you could always take off layers, but you couldn't put them on if you didn't wear them. That was how he felt about his guns and the amount of ammunition with which they held. Fratto looked around asking, "So, where the hell did you guys put all the live ones? Where's Junior? Where is that little fucker at? Please tell me at least he didn't get shot."

One of the men responded, not wanting to but also at the same time had zero interest in keeping this man waiting. He said, "It would seem they were standing on those stools, sir, when they heard the gunfire, they either didn't have time or more likely weren't smart enough to get their stupid asses down. It looks like you pretty much sliced through every one of their heads."

"God, I would have thought I'd taught that kid better. Just because you need muscle does not mean that it needs to be an ignorant set of muscles. I mean, for the love of God, can someone really be that stupid?"

Junior sat up quickly, first aiming the gun at the two men standing on either side of the doorway. He fired off, shooting both guns, not holding anything back. He cut them open across the sternum and down to the gut and before his dad could bring up his rifled machine gun. Junior smiled, making eye contact with his dad, and fired off two more shots.

Chapter 14

When Charlie was close to the parking lot, he slowed down. The three of them all said, "What the fuck," when they saw the never-ending rounds of bullets coming from the machine gun. They didn't waste any time seeing how good the brakes on Mr. Twain's car were. The sedan slid to a stop, not interested at all in making them think for even a millisecond they were bad guy reinforcements showing up. Charlie could just barely see Fratto, but he knew damn well that was who was doing the shooting. If he was worried about his son getting shot, it was impossible to tell.

A second car pulled in on the opposite end of the parking lot. No one got out and Charlie was pretty sure that was because it was Bruno and the crew. His demons wouldn't be an issue to worry about if they walked into the bar and Fratto senior was still there. It would be absolute carnage if that was the case. Fratto wasn't going to show them any sympathy; they'd be dead on sight, something Charlie hadn't really thought of when revenge had come into play. If they were stupid enough to stay there, then they'd be stupid enough to die. There'd be no holding back, he knew, by Fratto and whatever demons he had in him were not going to be worried about killing four more guys.

The men from the back of the bar were coming around. When they did, that seemed to be exactly what the car had been awaiting. Gunfire erupted from the machine gun coming out of the rear. The lights of the muzzle flash showed them their faces. It

was Bruno, Lou, Sid, and Minty. They were smiling and couldn't
have looked more content. Charlie watched as the men fell one
by one. It seemed like a lifetime watching the men getting
slaughtered before they were all dead and lying in the gravel
driveway shot to shit and motionless. Charlie didn't have any
allegiance to these men...but they didn't deserve to be shot
blindly without knowing what was coming at them. Of course,
Charlie saw a still smoking machine gun mounted somehow out of
the rear of an SUV. Charlie thought it looked like something that
the terminator would have done.

Tim was watching all of this of course. Jim was also. Tim asked,
"Do we want to get involved in this or..."

Charlie didn't answer for a minute. He watched as the four of
them exited the car, armed to the teeth and ready to finish off
anyone left in the bar who wasn't paying their salaries. Charlie
said, "Well if you want to get out then I'd do it now."

Jim said, "Well...we weren't going to get out, but if you fail at this
and we are just standing here I don't think that's going to go so
well. I mean we are good shots with shotguns and pistols, but
these guys are on a..."

"Shut up, Jim. Charlie, if you wanna go then do it. What do you
want us to do?"

"Put on your seatbelt...now!"

No one asked any questions and before they could click it, Charlie buried his foot into the pedal not leaving any leeway. He let off the brake and the car took off like a fucking bullet. Tim and Jim immediately began fumbling for their belts. This was in no way what he had been expecting in any way whatsoever. He turned on his brights, ensuring Bruno and his guys wouldn't be able to see what or who was coming at them. By the time they realized the car wasn't racing away from the gunfire but towards it, it was too late; there was nothing they could do other than fire directly at them. Jim screamed from the backseat when the bullets tore apart the windshield.

They tried their best to relax knowing that the impact was going to hurt...it was going to be fucking brutal as hell. The luxury sedan smashed into their vehicle. Bruno was at the wheel, and to be honest, Charlie would have not felt any different regardless of who was in that car driving. There were no innocents in it.

Tim was pretty sure he already knew the answer but felt warranted in the fact that he should probably still ask. He thought it seemed justifiable given the fact that when he looked down at the speedometer that even though the sedan was large as shit, it sure as hell was powered by something gigantic under the hood. Charlie had the car going 50-plus miles per hour and was pretty sure that he did not know what the outcome was going to be when they made it to their destination, which was approaching fucking quickly. Charlie also didn't seem to be doing anything but increasing their speed. Tim asked as nervously as Charlie had ever heard the man sound saying, "Are you going to slow down at any point?"

Charlie was more than over this day. He wanted it to end, to be done, and to go home so he could scrub whatever remaining cement off of his legs and go to sleep for a fucking week. Charlie smiled, looking like a neurotic psychopath saying, "Oh yeah, I'm slowing down real soon."

Tim didn't feel any more at ease by that statement asking, "When you say that, I gotta ask is that because you'll use the brakes, or is it going to be because of a crash keeping us from going any further forward?"

Charlie didn't need to answer, the car was but feet away by the time he'd finished asking his second question. That answer became self-evident when the beautiful, or once beautiful, car that Mr. Twain had probably treated a hell of a lot better than Charlie had collided, never slowing down into Bruno's side of their vehicle.

Jim, who was already in tremendous pain, was not looking forward to that which he knew was coming next. The three of them could all see Bruno and Minty's eyes in the front and rear seat looking like they were trying to figure out how in the hell they could get out of the vehicle in time but knew that there was absolutely no chance that would happen. The force from the car caved in the driver and rear passenger door three feet. The solid steel of Twain's American-made car didn't slow down until it had already done its damage. The airbags in the front and rear seats deployed on both cars. But unlike Charlie and his crew, Bruno's did not make the wisest of choices. Their vehicle reacted to no one's surprise instantaneously sending them rolling over and over again. Charlie lost count after the first four rotations of their vehicle. Charlie held their steering wheel straight, letting off the gas, finally slamming on the brakes and pulling the emergency brake at the same time. He was pretty sure if the windows had been down, they would be smelling frying brakes getting hotter and hotter by the second. Bruno's other mistake, or one of many, was they were so busy shooting that they weren't able to do that and have a seatbelt on. So, when they were rolling, they were being tossed around violently, worse by the second and bloodier as well.

When they finally came to a sliding stop, they sat there for just a moment and Charlie could feel tears in his eyes. He knew that he wasn't crying from fear but from pain. He was thinking what difference was it going to make if he now had a broken nose as well. It seemed to be the popular thing going on in the Keys lately. Charlie murmured, "Is everyone okay?"

Tim didn't say anything; he just groaned. Jim said, "Yeah, I'm fucking great. Minus this bullet that I think is either in my shoulder, or the trunk...it might have passed through."

This made Charlie and Tim's problems seem a little less important at the moment. On account that Jim now had a new hole in his body that he'd not begun the day with. Tim fumbled, getting his seatbelt off, and rolling up on his knees to look back at Jim who definitely had gotten the worst of it out of the three of them. His shirt had a telltale sign of being shot given the hole and the fact there must not have been a shortage of blood as his chest was growing more crimson by the second. Tim looked at the splattered blood on the rear window of the car which made Tim think it might have gone in and out. It would be yet to be told if that was true but typically blood only went on a rear windshield when it went through the body. Gunfire erupted again. The three of them ducked thinking that the gunfire was coming from Bruno's now totaled car.

Jim whispered, "They're twenty feet away. How the hell are they firing at us and missing?"

Tim replied, "Did you see them rolling? They probably got their fucking brains shook loose."

Charlie was gaining his senses back before they were. He said it as plain as though it was a fact, "That wasn't from them. It was the bar. Fratto's gotta be in there."

"You hear gunshots and that's what you think a good idea is to run inside?" Tim questioned, not feeling an amazing amount of faith in that move.

Charlie motioned saying, "Give me the shotgun. I'm going in."

"What do you want me to do if Bruno and them come out of that SUV? You leaving me with gimpy Jim here doesn't fill me with a helluva lot of confidence."

"I'm sorry that my body got in the way of the fucking machine guns. Maybe next time we can be lucky enough to know that they're going to start shooting at us. I've heard that there are these bulletproof vests. If we are going to keep this crap up, then we might invest in some."

Tim was going to say something else, but Charlie had reached for the gun, sliding out of the driver's seat. He raced inside, unsure what he would be able to do if those shots had been meant for Fratto senior. Charlie checked the action, making damn sure a shell was ready to go, and when he saw the black shell, he felt a sense of safety. Charlie didn't care what anyone had inside because a few well-placed birdshot shells would always take care of what was in front of it. There was little hiding from something that would paint an entire room.

Charlie had heard two bursts of gunfire. It didn't take a genius to know what that was. But, when he heard two single shots, those seemed to be aimed and if he had to guess they'd been shot with a purpose. He came through the doors that had been shattered and shot to shit anyway. It made his entry a little bit easier, which given the circumstances, he was quite alright with. Charlie looked around, not particularly in love with everything that he saw. With the exception of Fratto senior, Fratto's men, and Junior, they'd all been absolutely shot to shit. Their heads had been more or less cut down the middle.

Charlie saw Junior covered in sweat, his shirt sticking to him as well as his long black hair hanging wild. He looked like he'd been plucked out of The Grudge. Junior was smiling as he rose to his knees. Charlie still couldn't understand how in the hell a little peckerwood was alive given the very simple fact that the bar had appeared to have had thousands upon thousands of bullets riddling through this shitty old building. Charlie didn't say a word when he saw Junior. The last thing he wanted to do was get the attention of a mad man with two machine guns.

Junior was walking up towards his dad, hyper-focused on him, and for what Charlie could tell, only him. Junior said, "Didn't think I'd amount to anything. How many times have you told me that, pops? Now, look at you. A couple of bullet wounds and now it's just a matter of time, and you're dead, finally you'll be fucking dead. Hell, I can even tell the cops when they get here that I was trying to save your life. It's only going to be my word against...well, nobody. I mean given the fact that everyone's going to be fucking dead. Sounds like your reinforcements got taken out by some late backup. Probably, the only part of my new crew who seemed to be worth a shit. I guess they'll be getting raises."

Fratto was holding his hand over his neck and the other on his stomach. Charlie could see a decent flow of blood seeping through his fingers. It definitely did not take a genius to decipher that he was in an immense deal of pain and was not looking so hot. Charlie wondered if he was going to survive the night, given he got help. He couldn't believe that he was still sitting up and that he was still conscious. Fratto yelled, "You aren't anything but a piece of shit. Do you hear me? You laid there like a fucking pussy, trapping me and then shooting me. If you were a man, you would have already been up and coming at me. That Ford kid has more balls than you!"

Junior couldn't stand to hear his dad talk better about someone that he did not even know. He yelled, "Ford can go fuck himself!"

Charlie, who wasn't the biggest fan of people talking shit about him, scared both of the Frattos. He'd been silent and out of their views. He didn't care if he was a piece of shit, he still didn't appreciate hearing it. He said, "You know it's not nice to talk shit about someone that you don't really know, Junior. See, you had my uncle killed, tried to have me killed, and then as if that wasn't bad enough, you tried to have my fucking friends killed. For what, because you're too stupid to come up with your own drug routes or whatever the fuck my Uncle Joe was doing for your dad?"

Fratto actually looked a bit relieved seeing a thirty-inch barrel shotgun shouldered and ready, not waiting for Junior to point his first. Charlie could not see an intelligent reason why Fratto senior would have an issue with him shooting Junior, but not assuming would keep Charlie from making an ass out of himself and Fratto. Charlie said, "He needs to put those guns down, sir. If not, will everything that I need to do next be all right by you?"

Fratto replied without having to think about it saying, "I just need to preferably be the one that finishes him off. But there's only so much that I'm able to do."

Junior said, "This pretty boy isn't taking me out, Goddammit!"

Junior thought he was being quick, but Charlie was already well aware what was going to have to happen next. Charlie only fired once because that was all that he'd need to do. Junior screamed at the top of his lungs, dropping the pistol in his right hand not really able to fathom especially exactly what it was that he was looking at. The discharge had landed at least fifty hot pellets in his right hand. They quite literally had burned their way into his knuckles, hand, and his fingers. Each of them was busy blistering and bubbling, basically boiling his skin from the inside out. A pretty grotesque thing to see, Charlie had to admit. But he would rather see that than himself missing his shot and being killed because of his miss.

Junior's eyes filled with tears. No one could blame him and coincidentally no one felt bad for him either. Junior murmured belligerent, "You…you…you fuckin shot me!"

Charlie shrugged, never lowering his barrel, "Yeah, that's kind of what you do when someone fires a fucking machine gun at you and misses."

Junior said, "So this time I'm not going to…"

Charlie fired off a second shot, making it so someone else was gonna have to be opening Junior's pickles jars going forward. That is, if he survived this day. He screamed as loudly the second time as the first. It was deservingly so, given the fact that the second one looked even worse than the first if that was possible. Junior dropped the second gun at his feet. He looked like he was going to run. Fratto asked coolly and calmly, "Please keep my son here for me, Charlie."

Charlie motioned with his shotgun and Fratto nodded. Charlie took his last shot of the night aiming in between Junior's kneecaps and struck both of them. A handful of pellets went into each knee and he dropped to his knees, only for an instant because that hurt even worse than when he had been shot. He rolled over, falling, and ending up on his back. Unlike his dad, he did not have the opportunity to use his hands to try and make the pain, which was never-ending and racing throughout his body, feel less horrific. He waited for the pain to cease or even let up a bit, but it wasn't possible, and it didn't happen.

Fratto senior whispered, "Charlie, get me up."

"I think you could use a doctor, Mr. Fratto."

"I think it's Anthony, now. You saved my ass, kid."

"I'm gonna stick with Mr. Fratto, but sir, you do need an ambulance and a doctor."

"Tell you what Ford, get me to my feet and let me finish this night from hell. Then I'll make the call. I got someone on payroll. Kind of like Mr. Twain, who I'm god damned glad you aren't still with because I'd be dead. How's that sound?"

"Like you are ignoring the fact that you should probably not get up."

"If I needed your opinion, Charlie, then I'd ask for it."

Charlie walked over, ignoring Junior crying out in pain, pleading for mercy. He pulled Mr. Fratto up, letting him take a moment to steady himself. Charlie kept a firm grip on his bicep. The man was fighting not to show the pain. It wasn't a luxury that he allowed himself. Junior held up his bloodied, burned hands. He said, "Dad, dad, please don't, I'm sorry. We can work things out...we will be okay."

Fratto shook his head no. He said, "I don't have a son anymore. You're dead to me...quite literally."

Charlie was watching everything unfolding. He knew that everything that would happen next was going to be out of his control. There wasn't anything left for him to do but wait this out. "Dad, we can..."

Fratto pulled the trigger once, shooting Junior in the gut. He used his massacred hands to try and hold the wound. Charlie was going to ask him if he missed, but when he sent a shot every three inches going up his sternum, he realized he was aiming and hitting exactly where he wanted to strike him. After the third shot, Charlie was pretty sure that Junior was no longer, but that didn't seem to stop Fratto senior. He didn't stop firing until he'd worked his way all the way up to his brain. Fratto stood looking at his kid and wishing it hadn't come to this. But since it did, this was the way he would prefer it ended. Fratto reached in, pulling out a handkerchief and wiping his prints, which he knew would be difficult to pull anyways and walked over, putting the firearm into the hand of one of his men.

Fratto started to fall face first. Charlie dropped the shotgun, running over, swooping him up and put him down into a chair. He said, "Hey, where's your phone. Let's get that doctor called, what's he under in your phone?"

Fratto pulled it out of his pocket. He said, "I don't know how much longer I'm going to be awake for. Please call Mr. Kenny, hopefully he's available."

"Isn't he like Mr. Twain, also on call?"

"Yes, but that doesn't mean he isn't dealing with the water of life."

"Sir?"

"He's Scottish. It's what they call whiskey. I'm just hoping he's coherent."

"Do you want me to drive you there?"

"Charlie, make the call, please, son."

Charlie made the call and when a man with as thick of an accent as he'd ever heard answered the man said, "Hello, Mr. Fratto, I hope you're calling to come have a drink with me."

"Is this line secure?"

"Who is this?"

"Sir, I don't have time to waste, is this…"

"Stop asking stupid questions if time is of the essence, why do you have Mr. Fratto's phone?"

"Because he's been shot, twice. He told me to call you right before he passed out."

When Kenny heard this, he regretfully set his whiskey down, getting up, and started walking for the door. He absolutely hated doing this to himself but knew that if he needed to drive then it'd be important that he get there without killing himself. Kenny reached in his pocket, finding a 'for emergency use only' vial and opening it, sticking it beneath his nostril and taking a big ol' snort. The smelling salts felt like they gripped onto his foggy brain as if it were a wet towel and wrung out every ounce of booze he had in him. Kenny yelled, startling Charlie saying, "That'll wake you up in the mornin' boys!"

"Are you okay?"

"I am now. Jesus Christ, that'll make your nipples harder than ice. Send me a message where you want me. I'll be there as soon as I can. It just depends on how far you are away."

"I'm in the Keys, do you know Junior's bar?"

"Yes, I've been there more than once having to give some shots so special itches go away. That damn kid, between us, never seemed to have the common sense that he needed to stick his pecker where it wouldn't need to worry about falling off afterward, if you know what I mean?"

"It isn't a pretty sight. I won't lie."

"I've seen some horrible shit. Can I do this with a car, or should I bring my mobile office?"

"I don't know, probably the mobile office. His pulse isn't too damn strong. He looks like shit, too."

"Well, that usually happens once someone gets shot."

Charlie couldn't disagree. He was going to say something else but looked down seeing the call had ended. Charlie kept Fratto in the chair and did his best to come up with some makeshift bandages. By the time Kenny got there, Charlie was genuinely concerned for his well-being. Tim had brought Jim in with his help. Jim wasn't looking too hot, and Charlie wasn't loving any of this. He was really hoping that the doctor would help Jim as well.

It didn't seem to take too long, and two things showed up...actually three. Detective Lindvall came into the bar. He had his gun out and ready already. He stopped in his tracks when he saw Fratto on the ground, Junior shot to shit, and Jim with a new hole in his arm. Lindvall stood for a few moments, trying to piece everything together and what he should do next. He motioned to Senior asking, "Is he gonna live?"

"A doctor is on his way."

"Good thing. Jimbo over there and Senior both look like a bag of shit."

Jim said, "Well, maybe if I could get shot a second time I would look almost as ugly as you."

Lindvall was shaking his head. He wasn't going to get in a pissing match; it wouldn't do anything for him. He said, "I saw Bruno and his crew out in the car. They look like if they get an ambulance that they might have a chance of making it...at least a few of them. Sid seemed to catch a gunshot to the head, probably from one of his own crew...fucking idiot. What am I going to do with you, Ford? Are you going to take that fancy boat of yours and find somewhere new to live?"

"I wasn't planning on leaving anytime soon."

"Just stay out of my way, Ford, or you're going to wish that you did."

Charlie smiled, saying, "Just remember I've got something saved for safekeeping. Get out of here. When Fratto comes around, you might not want to be someone associated with Junior's place. I don't think he's going to be too kind."

"How long are you going to hold that over my head?"

"Depends, how long do you plan on working?"

"Until I hit my twenty years or make a sweet score."

"Says the dirty cop. Just do me a favor. I'll stay out of your way, Lindvall, and you stay out of my life. Does that seem like a deal?"

"I'll do my best; just don't forget what you are saying."

"What about Bruno and his crew?"

"They'll be going to jail for a minute. Unlike you three, I don't think there'll be much difficulty with their charges sticking. I can think of a few million things we could put on them. Their employer won't be making their monthly payment to keep them in the lifestyle that they prosper from."

"I thought they worked for Nydegger Esquire?"

"Yeah, and they do. But I don't think his employer is going to need him for too much either."

Lindvall didn't say anything else. He turned around, standing sideways and letting in someone Charlie didn't know. Which was something he was used to. Charlie looked the man over, seeing a white guy that appeared to be in his late thirties without much hair, but unlike Charlie, didn't seem to be a choice. One thing for this doctor didn't scream walking in was that he was a doctor. He didn't say anything but walked right towards Fratto, a poker face came over him and he knew that this guy appeared to know his shit and what to do. He ripped Fratto's shirt open and assessed what needed to be done.

Jim said, "Any chance you can take a look at me, doc, when you are done?"

"You one of Fratto's guys?"

Charlie said, "Otherwise I can give Twain a call and see if he is available. Hopefully he has another car, that one outside is pretty fucked up."

"You know Fratto and Twain. It seems like if you aren't, then you should be."

Jim replied, "Just sitting here leaking blood, doc."

Two guys dressed somewhat like medics came in with a gurney and oxygen. Kenny said, "Get him on here, get him started with his back up blood and I'll be there in a minute. Everything looks like it went through clean. It should just be blood loss, nothing important was hit, just meat."

He walked over to Jim taking a quick look. He was less worried about Jim than Fratto. Mostly this was because he got paid by Fratto and didn't know this guy from a stranger on the street. He checked the wound and said, "Oh Christ, you're fine. You won't even bleed out from this. If you aren't guilty or on the run for anything, just go to the hospital. Otherwise, you're going to need to wait quite a few hours while I work on Fratto."

"Glad to know where I fall on the food chain."

"You aren't even ant shit on the chain, son. You drop me the kind of figures Fratto does, and I could have you taken care of in no time, but you don't look like you've got a helluva lot of money to throw around. Don't worry though, the hospital is forced to take you and treat you."

"I'm a vet, I got insurance for life."

"That's wonderful," Kenny said as they headed out of the bar alongside the gurney. "If you want to swing by, I can make sure the vet doctors didn't fuck anything up for you."

Tim got Jim up to his feet. Charlie said, "Sounds like we need to take Jim to the hospital. I was ready for bed, and here you go trying to stop bullets with your shoulder. What the hell were you thinking?"

"Charlie, can you come just a little closer?" Jim asked.

"Sure, if you want me to be on your left side. I wouldn't want you freaking out and making a bad choice, friend."

Jim replied, "Well that's pretty smart if I do say so myself. I mean overall. But really, just come here please, I'd like to give you a hug."

They got to their feet and headed out; Jim knew Charlie was just busting his balls. When they got outside, a news crew was there and stopped them as they were walking to the closest SUV. Charlie decided the one that had the machine gun should probably be left here. He didn't think that Fratto had too many issues with the ability to be able to get a new one. A lady stopped them saying, "Sirs, could you tell me please what happened, tonight?"

Charlie and Tim both said, "No comment, ma'am."

The woman who was just passing thirty years old said, "That's cute, I am so not a ma'am."

Jim smiled, saying, "No, she's an absolute fox. Maybe it is the blood loss that's making me a bit ditzy, but I'm pretty sure that this woman should have my baby."

She blushed, trying to get her bearings back. She realized the bloodied man should be her go to for questions. The news reporter said, "My name is Karen Dziegiel with Channel 2 News. I'm just trying to get the people the facts. They are worried about what is happening tonight."

Jim said, "Well, good for you ma'am. We are all safe and so are you. You are way too good looking to be getting messed up. See, we were driving by, and these mad men were shooting all of the men on the inside and outside of the club. We decided it'd be our civic duty to help those poor men. So, we crashed into their car. That was the end of their shooting."

"Oh, that sounds horribly dangerous."

"Oh, it was sweetheart. But luckily, we are all ex-Navy and couldn't be scared by a few thousand rounds of gunfire coming our way. We slammed right into them. We had been looking for the guys who killed his Uncle Joe and led us here."

"Wait, are you private detectives?"

"Yes, we could be, absolutely."

"No, we sure as hell aren't," Charlie said.

Jim said, "You can call us at 515-915-2311 ask for Charlie, he owes us and will need to take the calls until we get a secretary."

Karen said, "Uh, sounds like these three are heroes and taking care of things the Key's Police haven't been able to handle. Keep up with Channel 2 for the most recent news on this and other events."

Charlie wanted to strangle him. However, he didn't want to do that until he was taken care of at the hospital. Tim was in the same boat. There were currently plenty of extra SUVs sitting around waiting for owners who weren't going to come. The three picked one not riddled with bullet holes and when they got into the SUV, Tim asked, "Are you on some type of drugs by chance, Jim, when the hell did we talk about doing that?"

"I just kind of thought of it. We need a job, and we have a boat. We know how to handle ourselves. If we could skip getting shot, then we would be really able to kick some ass. If you know what I mean."

"I think that I'd like to kick your ass, Jim," Tim replied.

"Just get me to the hospital so I can get sewn up. You'll thank me later."

Charlie said, "Not today I won't."

To Be continued

By Mike Evans

A quick note from the author, if you enjoyed this book I would very much appreciate you taking a minute to head to Amazon to review this book, or at the least give it a star rating, please. Clicking this will take you to review.

Please see below for additional info by Mike Evans
Mike's newsletter don't miss out on any news!
http://www.tinyurl.com/evansnews

Mike Evans Facebook Author Page
https://www.facebook.com/MikeEvansAuthor

Contact Email
m.evansauthor@gmail.com

Mike Evans on Amazon
https://www.amazon.com/Mike-Evans/e/B00IQ9Z75A

Do you love an action book?

Charlie Ford Adventure Series

Gabriel Series

Buried: Broken oaths

The Operator

Want zombies?

Vacation from Hell Series

Zombies on The Block Series

The Orphans Series

Zombies and Chainsaws Series

Looking for some true-crime style serial killer fiction?

The Uninvited Series

Voices in My Head

Are the devil, demons, and holy wars your thing?

Demons Beware Series

Deal with The Devil